INTERIOR CHINATOWN

INTERIOR CHINATOWN

★ ★ ★

CHARLES YU

★ ★ ★

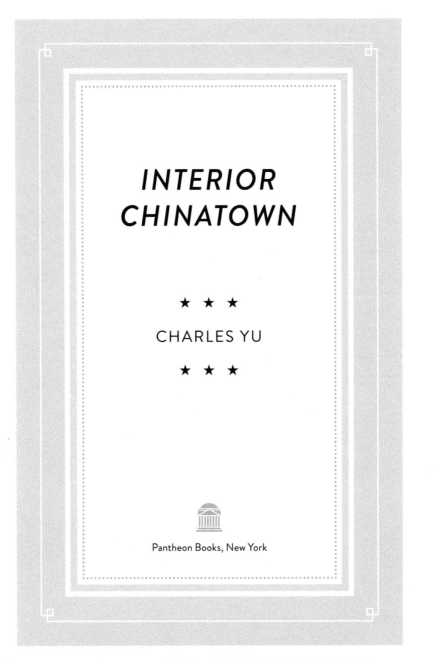

Pantheon Books, New York

Copyright © 2020 by Charles Yu

All rights reserved. Published in the United States by Pantheon Books,
a division of Penguin Random House LLC, New York, and distributed in
Canada by Penguin Random House Canada Limited, Toronto.

Pantheon Books and colophon are registered trademarks of
Penguin Random House LLC.

Library of Congress Cataloging-in-Publication Data
Name: Yu, Charles, [date] author.
Title: Interior Chinatown / Charles Yu.
Description: First edition. New York : Pantheon Books, 2020.
Identifiers: LCCN 201901427. ISBN 9780307907196
(hardcover : alk. paper). ISBN 9780307907202 (ebook).
Classification: LCC PS3625.U15 I58 2020 | DDC 813/.6—dc23 |
LC record available at lccn.loc.gov/2019014271

www.pantheonbooks.com

Jacket design by Tyler Comrie

Printed in the United States of America
First Edition

2   4   6   8   9   7   5   3   1

For Sophia and Dylan

INTERIOR CHINATOWN

Charles Yu

125

If a film needed an exotic backdrop . . . Chinatown could be made to represent itself or any other Chinatown in the world. Even today, it stands in for the ambiguous Asian anywhere.

Bonnie Tsui

ACT I

GENERIC ASIAN MAN

INT. GOLDEN PALACE

Ever since you were a boy, you've dreamt of being
Kung Fu Guy.

You are not Kung Fu Guy.

You are currently Background Oriental Male, but
you've been practicing.

Maybe tomorrow will be the day.

INT. GOLDEN PALACE

Ever since you were a boy, you've dreamt of being
Kung Fu Guy.

You are not Kung Fu Guy.

You are currently Oriental Guy Making a Weird
Face, but you've been practicing.

Maybe tomorrow will be the day.

Take what you
can get.

Try to build
a life.

A life
at the
margin

made from
bit parts.

WILLIS WU

(ASIAN) ACTOR

Skills:

Kung Fu (Moderate Proficiency)

Fluent in Accented English

Able to do Face of Great Shame on command

Résumé/Repertoire:

Disgraced Son

Delivery Guy

Silent Henchman

Caught Between Two Worlds

Guy Who Runs in and Gets Kicked in the Face

Striving Immigrant

Generic Asian Man

Your mother has played, in no particular order:

Pretty Oriental Flower
Asiatic Seductress
Young Dragon Lady
Slightly Less Young Dragon Lady
Restaurant Hostess
Girl with the Almond Eyes
Beautiful Maiden Number One
Dead Beautiful Maiden Number One
Old Asian Woman

Your father has been, at various times:

Twin Dragon
Wizened Chinaman
Guy in a Soiled T-shirt
Inscrutable Grocery Owner (in a Soiled T-shirt)
Egg Roll Cook
Young Asian Man
Sifu, the Mysterious Kung Fu Master
Old Asian Man

INT. GOLDEN PALACE—MORNING

In the world of Black and White, everyone starts
out as Generic Asian Man. Everyone who looks like
you, anyway. Unless you're a woman, in which case
you start out as Pretty Asian Woman.

You all work at Golden Palace, formerly Jade
Palace, formerly Palace of Good Fortune. There's
an aquarium in the front and cloudy tanks of rock
crabs and two-pound lobsters crawling over each
other in the back. Laminated menus offer the lunch
special, which comes with a bowl of fluffy white
rice and choice of soup, egg drop or hot and sour.
A neon Tsingtao sign blinks and buzzes behind the
bar in the dimly lit space, a dropped-ceiling room
with lacquered ornate woodwork (or some imitation
thereof), everything simmering in a warm, seedy
red glow thrown off by the dollar-store paper
lanterns festooned above, many of them darkened by
dead moths, the paper yellowing, ripped, curling in
on itself.

The bar is fully stocked with top-shelf spirits
up top, middle-shelf liquor at eye level, and down
at the bottom, a happy hour shelf of booze that
you will regret for sure. The new thing everyone
is excited about is called the lychee margarita-
tini, which seems like a lot of flavors. Not that
you've had one. They're fourteen bucks. Sometimes
patrons leave a sip at the bottom of the glass and
if you're quick, while you go through the swinging
door that separates the front of the house from
the back, you can have a taste—you've seen some
of the other Generic Asian Men do it. It's a risk,

though. The director's always got an eye out, ready
to fire someone for the smallest infraction.

You wear the uniform: white shirt, black pants.
Black slipperlike shoes that have no traction
whatsoever. Your haircut is not good, to say the
least.

Black and White always look good. A lot of it
has to do with the light. They're the heroes. They
get hero lighting, designed to hit their faces just
right. Designed to hit White's face just right,
anyway.

Someday you want the light to hit your face like
that. To look like the hero. Or for a moment to
actually be the hero.

ROLES

First, you have to work your way up. Starting from
the bottom, it goes:

   5. Background Oriental Male

   4. Dead Asian Man

   3. Generic Asian Man Number Three/Delivery Guy

   2. Generic Asian Man Number Two/Waiter

   1. Generic Asian Man Number One

and then if you make it that far (hardly anyone
does) you get stuck at Number One for a while and
hope and pray for the light to find you and that
when it does you'll have something to say and
when you say that something it will come out just
right and have everyone in Black and White turning
their heads saying wow who is that, that is not

just some Generic Asian Man, that is a star, maybe
not a real, regular star, let's not get crazy,
we're talking about Chinatown here, but perhaps
a Very Special Guest Star, which for your people
is the ceiling, is the terminal, ultimate, exalted
position for any Asian working in this world, the
thing every Oriental Male dreams of when he's in
the Background, trying to blend in.

Kung Fu Guy.

Kung Fu Guy is not like the other slots in the
hierarchy—there isn't always someone occupying
the position, as in whoever the top guy is at any
given time, that's the default guy who gets trotted
out whenever there's kung fu to be done. Only a
very special Asian can be worthy of the title.
It takes years of dedication and sacrifice, and
after all that only a few have even a slim chance
of making it. Despite the odds, you all grew up
training for this and only this. All the scrawny
yellow boys up and down the block dreaming the
same dream.

INT. GOLDEN PALACE

Ever since you were a boy, you've dreamt of being
Kung Fu Guy.
  You are still not Kung Fu Guy.
  You are currently Generic Asian Man Number
Three/Delivery Guy. Your kung fu is B, B-plus on
a good day, and Sifu once proclaimed your drunken
monkey to be nearly at a level of competence that
he could perhaps at some point in the future
imagine not being completely embarrassed of you.
Which, if you know him, well, that's a pretty big
deal.
  To be honest though it can sometimes be hard
to tell with Sifu, who is famously inscrutable.
If you could only show him what you've become.
All you want is for him to make that face, the
one that looks like internal distress possibly of
a gastrointestinal nature but actually indicates
something closer to Deeply Repressed Secret Pride
Honorable Father Has for His Young but Promising
Son; means Deliciously Bittersweet Pain That
Comes from Knowing Honorable Teacher Is No Longer
Needed. That's how you see it in your head: he
would make that face, smile, you'd smile back.
Credits roll and you'd walk off, arm in arm, to the
horizon.

OLD ASIAN MAN

These days he is mostly Old Asian Man. No longer
Sifu, with the pants and the muscles and the look

in his eye. All of that is gone now, but when did
it happen? Over years and overnight.

The day you first noticed. You'd shown up a few
minutes early for weekly lesson. Maybe that's what
threw him off. When he answered the door, it took
him a moment to recognize you. Two seconds, or
twenty, a frozen eternity—then, as he regained
himself, his familiar scowl, barking your name

WILLIS WU!

half-exclamation, half-confirmation, as if
verifying for both you and himself that he hadn't
forgotten. Willis Wu, he said again, well come on,
what are you doing, don't just stand there in the
doorway like a dum-dum, come in, son, let's get
started.

He was fine for the rest of the day, mostly, but
you couldn't stop thinking about the look he gave
you, oblivion or terror, and for the first time you
noticed the mess his room had become, not unusual
for any other man his age living alone, but for
Sifu, who taught and valued order and simplicity in
all things, to have allowed his dwelling to reach
this state of disorganization should have been a
warning sign to all. Maybe not the first, but the
first one that came to your attention.

Fatty Choy went around telling everyone that
Sifu was on food stamps, saying how gullible can
you be ("You idiots think being Wizened Chinaman
pays well? Are you crazy? Why do you think he
fishes bottles and cans out of the trash?") but
no one wanted to believe it. At least in public.

In private, the thought did occur. Sifu never had
the lights on. Said it was to train the senses.
He saved everything: disposable chopsticks, free
glossy calendars from East-West Bank ("good for
wrapping fish or fruit"), packets of soy sauce
and chili paste from the dollar Chinese down the
street. He'd patched his old fake leather couch so
many times there were cracks on the patches. Which
of course he also patched. The Formica two-top he
ate on was the first and only kitchen table he'd
ever bought, purchased for seven dollars and fifty
cents from the salvage bin at the old restaurant
supply warehouse down on Jackson and Eighth,
that place long gone now (converted to INT. RAVE/
GRIMY CLUB SCENE) but the table still there in
the kitchen. An artifact of the previous century,
it had worn down to a smoothness so comforting
and cool it felt soft to the touch, the patterns
of use, hundreds, thousands of meals together in
the corner of that small, low-ceilinged room, the
surface preserving the teachings of Sifu, wisdom
over time recorded in the warp and wear, in the
markings of the modest table itself. Come to
think of it, Fatty Choy, despite the fact that
he was and had always been a total gasbag, a
mostly insufferable close-talking blowhard (made
all the more insufferable by the fact that he was
not infrequently right about things), was simply
stating what you all knew but didn't want to admit:
Sifu had gotten old.

It was easy to lie to yourself about it. Although
naively you believed he had by some miracle of
genetics and sheer follicular willpower managed

to reach his seventh decade without a single hair
turning gray, in hindsight you remember once
seeing an empty box of natural seaweed coloring in
his wastebasket, Sifu emerging from his room with
the occasional smear where he'd gotten a little
careless and ended up painting the top edge of his
forehead a swath of kelpish green.

And even if he could still break a cinder block
with three fingers, that was nothing compared to
back in the day, his younger self, when he could
do it with just one—a single powerful blow of
any digit. You pick! You couldn't bear to watch,
peeking through your fingers when you were little,
and as you got older still wincing in expectation
of painful failure. But young Sifu never failed.
He always found the necessary reserves of qi, was
able to summon forth from whatever intangible
reservoir the required force to smash through
it, and everyone gathered around would clap and
shout their praise at the latest demonstration of
Sifu's mind over matter, mental and physical, an
impossible feat right there in the alley behind the
kitchen in the middle of a Tuesday. At the sound
of the exploding energy you would uncover your
eyes and exhale with relief, proud and grateful
that he had done it once again, hadn't mangled his
hand, and also slightly ashamed by your lack of
faith, when everyone else, the assembled friends
and strangers, had never doubted him in the
slightest.

Your earliest memories of him as a young dragon,
a rising star, thick straight hair the color of
night combed slowly and carefully straight back

in a lustrous wave. Forearms like steel barrels lifting you out of the makeshift playpen in the corner of the room and flying you around up above his head, almost crashing into the bed and the lamp and the ceiling as you laughed and laughed until your mother said *sio sim, sio sim,* that's enough, Ming, please, stop before he gets sick, and he'd do one more revolution before setting you down safely, your feet back on solid ground, the world still spinning.

Whether we admitted to it or not, and sometimes you did admit it to yourself, right before falling asleep, in the way thoughts like this come to you: your first, best, and only real master, the source of all your kung fu knowledge, was no longer himself. He'd aged out of his role and into the next one, his life force depleting with every exertion. Wisdom and power leaking from him with each passing day and night. He'd played his role for so long he'd lost himself in it, before some separation that happened gradually over decades and then you waking one day to feel it, some distance that had crept in overnight. Some formal space you could no longer cross.

He'd always be Your Father, but somehow was no longer your dad.

No longer running up walls, no more leaping from the curved roof eaves of the Bank of America pagoda. More often found nodding off during a meal, eaten alone, in front of the six o'clock news. Long after you'd graduated into an adult role, you still continued coming to him for these weekly lessons, but the lessons had turned into a

flimsy pretense layered atop their real purpose:
your delivery of provisions on which your old
man depended. A few groceries, toilet paper, his
various prescriptions. Putting things out so they'd
be easy for him to access, wiping the floor as best
you could. There was only so much time. Checking
for dampness on his mattress pad, changing it if
necessary, picking up laundry, sweeping from his
nightstand the accumulation of balled-up napkins
enclosing clots of dried phlegm and blood. More
napkins behind the nightstand and all around, a
half-eaten pear under the Formica table, there
since the day after your last visit, having dropped
and rolled to a stop right in that very spot, left
to slowly rot, the gentle descent into squalor not
a function of sloth but simple, physical inability.

I'm sorry. I can't reach.

It's okay, Ba. I got it.

The apologies, the true sign—that this was not
the man you once knew, a man who would never
have uttered that word to his son, sorry, and in
English, no less. Not because he thought himself
infallible, but because of his belief that a family
should never have to say sorry, or please, or thank
you, for that matter, these things being redundant,
being contradictory to the parent-son relationship,
needing to remain unstated always, these things
being the invisible fabric of what a family is.

You did what you could despite being generally
ignored. Sifu-now-Old-Asian-Man having forgotten
not just his kung fu technique but also his most
loyal student, regarding you with a blank if
slightly wary amiability, as one might endure an

overbearing but helpful stranger. Your relationship
having turned into a pantomime, a series of
gestures in a well-worn scene, played out again and
again, any underlying feeling having long since
been obviated by emotional muscle memory, learning
how to make the right faces, strike the right
poses, not out of apathy or lack of sincerity,
rather a need to preserve what was left of his
pride.

The trick was learning what not to say. To enter
the theater of his dotage quietly, sit there in
the dark and not ask him any question, however
simple, that might cause momentary confusion, might
turn your rote interactions into something too
raw, remind yourselves or each other of what was
happening here, the inversion of the relationship,
the care and feeding, the brute fact of physical
dependency: If you don't do this, he can't do it
for himself. If you miss a week, he sits in the
dark. Not that he'll die. Although there is always
that possibility. But he'll be lonelier that day,
hungrier. He'll lose something or drop something or
break something and have to wait for you to call
or come by. Staying in character avoided all of
that, allowed you to prolong your respective roles
for just a bit longer, and in a good week, when
things were going along relatively well, you could
get by, could walk through your blocking and lines,
make it to the end of the day. But on bad days or
if you'd stay too long, his patience or working
memory would reach its limit, and he'd edge into a
twilight distrust, fear in his eyes.

Even on the worst days, he never completely

forgot you for more than a minute or two—somehow in his paranoia you sensed he always knew that you were *someone* to him. You suspect that only made him more afraid of you, your presence a vague familiarity triggering in some deep part of his memory an inchoate, low-level anxiety, the son returning home, the lost son come to assert his right to challenge the father.

In the months since, he eventually settled into a new, diminished equilibrium, even began to work again, as Old Asian Cook or Old Asian Guy Smoking, which was rough, was a hard thing to see for anyone who'd known him back when. Known what he'd been capable of. A new role, a new phase of life, it could be a way of starting fresh, the slate wiped clean.

But the old parts are always underneath. Layers upon layers, accumulating. Which was the problem. No one in Chinatown able to separate the past from the present, always seeing in him (and in each other, in yourselves), all of his former incarnations, the characters he'd played in your minds long after the parts had ended.

In that way, Sifu had gotten this old without anyone noticing. Including your mother—deemed to have aged out of Asian Seductress, no longer Girl with the Almond Eyes, now Old Asian Woman—living down the hall, their marriage having entered its own dusky phase, bound for eternity but separate in life. The rationale being that she needed to continue to work in order to be able to support him and for that she needed a minimum amount of rest and peace of mind, all true, and that they

were better apart than together, also true. The
reality being that they'd lost the plot somewhere
along the way, their once great romance spun into
a period piece, into an immigrant family story, and
then into a story about two people trying to get
by. And it was just that: getting by. Barely, and
no more. Because they'd also, in the way old people
often do, slipped gently into poverty. Also without
anyone noticing.

Poor is relative, of course. None of you were
rich or had any dreams of being rich or even knew
anyone rich. But the widest gulf in the world is
the distance between getting by and not quite
getting by. Crossing that gap can happen in a
hundred ways, almost all by accident. Bad day at
work and/or kid has a fever and/or miss the bus
and consequently ten minutes late to the audition
which equals you don't get to play the part of
Background Oriental with Downtrodden Face. Which
equals, stretch the dollar that week, boil chicken
bones twice for a watery soup, make the bottom of
the bag of rice last another dinner or three.

Cross that gap and everything changes. Being
on this side of it means that time becomes your
enemy. You don't grind the day—the day grinds you.
With the passing of every month your embarrassment
compounds, accumulates with the inevitability of
a simple arithmetic truth. X is less than Y, and
there's nothing to be done about that. The daily
mail bringing with it fresh dread or relief, but
if the latter, only the most temporary kind,
restarting the clock on the countdown to the next
bill or past-due notice or collection agency call.

Sifu, like many others INT. CHINATOWN SRO, had without warning or complaint slid just under the line so quietly it was easy to minimize how painful it must have been. The pain of having once been young, with muscles, still able to work. To have lived an entire life of productivity, of self-sufficiency, having been a net giver, never a taker, never relying on others. To call oneself master, to hold oneself out as a source of expertise, to have had the courage and ability and discipline that added up to a meaningful, perhaps even noteworthy life, built over decades from nothing, and then at some point in that serious life, finding oneself searching for *calories*. Knowing what time of day the restaurant tosses its leftover steamed pork buns. Not in a position to turn down any food, however obtained, eyeing the markdown bins in the ninety-nine-cent store, full of dense, sugary bricks and slabs and disk-sized cookies, not food really, really only meant for children, something to fill the belly of a person who once took himself seriously. Buying this food without hesitation, necessity overcoming any shame in simply eating it, and not just eating it, swallowing it down more quickly than intended, a young man's dignity replaced by a newly acquired clumsiness, the hands and mouth and belly knowing what the heart and head had not yet come to terms with: hunger. Nothing like an empty stomach to remind you what you are.

To be fair, it wasn't as if anyone in Chinatown was in a great monetary position to be helping Sifu. Old Asian Woman did what she could, but as

work slowed down, had enough of a challenge trying
to take care of herself. And you just starting
out, contributing what you could manage, a bag of
food or medicine, once in a while a piece of fish
or meat. That's what you tell yourself anyway. The
truth being that if each of you had done a little,
together it might have been enough.

OLDER BROTHER

Some say that the person who should have helped
the most, was in a position to help the most,
having been Sifu's number-one-most-naturally-gifted-
kung-fu-superstar-in-training-pupil all those years
and thus having reaped the greatest benefit from
Sifu's teachings, was Older Brother.

Not your actual older brother. Better. Everyone's
Older Brother. The prodigy. The homecoming king.
Unofficial mayor of the neighborhood. Guardian of
Chinatown.

Once the heir apparent to Sifu, the two of
them even starring together in a brief but
notable project about father-and-son martial arts
experts (Logline: When political considerations
make conventional military tactics impossible,
the government calls on a highly secretive elite
special ops force—a father-son duo among the best
hand-to-hand fighters in the world—in order to get
the job done, Codename: TWIN DRAGONS).

Older Brother who never had to work his way up
the ladder, never had to be Generic Asian Man.
Older Brother who was born, bred, and trained to

be, and eventually did become, Kung Fu Guy, which
meant, of course, making Kung Fu Guy money,
which is good for your kind but still basically
falls under the general category of secondary
roles.

Older Brother.

Like Bruce Lee, but also completely different.

Lee being legendary, not mythical. Too real,
too specific to be a myth, the particulars of his
genius known and part of his ever-accumulating
personal lore. Electromuscular stimulation.
Ingesting huge quantities of royal jelly. And
with his development of his own discipline, Jeet
Kune Do, the creation of an entirely new fighting
system and philosophical worldview. Bruce Lee was
proof: not all Asian Men were doomed to a life of
being Generic. If there was even one guy who had
made it, it was at least theoretically possible
for the rest.

But easy cases make bad law, and Bruce Lee
proved too much. He was a living, breathing video
game boss-level, a human cheat code, an idealized
avatar of Asian-ness and awesomeness permanently
set on Expert difficulty. Not a man so much as a
personification, not a mortal so much as a deity
on loan to you and your kind for a fixed period
of time. A flame that burned for all yellow to
understand, however briefly, what perfection was
like.

Older Brother was the inverse.

Not a legend but a myth.

Or a whole bunch of myths, overlapping,
redundant, contradictory. A mosaic of ideas, a

thousand and one puzzle pieces that teased you, let you see the edges of something, clusters here and there, just enough to keep hope alive that the next piece would be the one, the answer snapping into place, showing how it all fit together.

Bruce Lee was the guy you worshipped. Older Brother was the guy you dreamt of growing up to be.

BEGIN OLDER BROTHER AWESOMENESS MONTAGE:

—Older Brother always has the good hair, not the kind that goes straight up and then out at weird angles and with stupid cowlicks in the back and on the side and wherever else. Not the kind that makes you think of math club and pocket protectors. Older Brother was blessed, among other things, with the rare phenotype, the kind of Asian dude hair with a slight wave to it (but always in a tight fade), thick and black but with brown or even red highlights.

—Older Brother's kung fu is A-plus-plus, obviously, but he isn't limited to just kung fu. He can also mess around with Muay Thai, is proficient in a couple forms of judo, and is definitely down with Taekwondo (and its many strip mall variations). His Brazilian grappling is legit if you care to go to ground with him, but you shouldn't because in about eight seconds you'll be tapping the mat, asking him through tears of excruciating pain to please stop bending your arm that way.

—If you get Older Brother drunk enough (not that
he ever really gets drunk, just sort of slightly
faded, Older Brother's legendary tolerance for
alcohol having been proven time and again in
countless drinking games and late-night wagers,
some fun, some not so fun) he will show you knife
tricks that will leave you laughing and scared
shitless at the same time and he will do it
effortlessly, knife in one hand, beer in the other,
his long hair looking cool.

—It's not clear if he can dunk (no one's ever seen
him try) but he can definitely grab the rim and
that alone is pretty impressive given that he's
five eleven and three-quarters.

—Which, for the record, is the perfect height for
an Asian dude. Tall enough for women to notice
(even in heels! even White women!), tall enough to
not get ignored by the bartender, but not so tall
to get called Yao Ming and considered some kind of
Mongolian freak.

—And if you get any ideas that you could take
him in a bar fight or on the basketball court
or anywhere else, you'll quickly find out the
hard way what a bad idea that is. Guys don't
want to fight him anyway—they call him Bruce
("Yo, yo, I've seen *Fists of Fury* like a hundred
times"), or Jackie or Jet Li, and he's cool with
it all, whatever the vibe, wherever it's coming
from. Everyone admired his level of comfort,
moving in and out of language and subculture, from

backroom poker game to dudes on the corner looking
for trouble to the octogenarians playing Go or
mahjong at the Benevolent Family Association. Older
Brother's reach and influence was not limited to
the Middle Kingdom and its ethnic diaspora, but
extended into other neighboring domains: he could
sing karaoke with the Japanese salarymen, could
polish off two plates of ddukbokki slathered in
a tangy, blood-red gochujang, wash it down with a
bottle of milky soju, all while beating the pants
off the K-town regulars at their own drinking
games, dropping some of his passable Korean (mostly
curse words) in the process.

—Older Brother was never in a gang, not even
close, makes a point of not even being loosely
affiliated with a triad or Wah Ching, yet somehow
manages it so that those scary dudes are still
cool with him. He gives them their distance and
they do the same with him, a form of silent
respect.

—On top of all this, Older Brother was a National
Merit Scholar. 1570 on the SAT.

—Everyone has their own story about Older Brother.

"Man you don't even know. Last week I saw him
at Jackson and Eleventh."
"What was he doing?"
"Chin-ups on the cross bar of the traffic
signal."
"I saw him, too."

"No you didn't."

"I did. He was doing them one-handed."

"No shit one-handed. OB doesn't mess around with regular chin-ups. Not like your weak sauce."

"You're weak sauce."

"Say that again. To my face."

"You're weak sauce."

"Shut up, idiots. Did one of you really see Older Brother?"

"Yeah. Like I said. Chin-ups. Did like fifty of them."

"More like seventy."

"With his left hand."

"He's left-handed, dumbass."

"Older Brother is left-handed? Come on. You're the dumbass, dumbass."

"He's ambidextrous. You're both dumbasses."

—That's pretty much how it goes with Older Brother stories piled on more stories, conflicting, combining, canceling each other out. In the end, you're not sure how much of it's real and how much is local lore, exploits that over the years have expanded, but in any case it doesn't matter. Even if Older Brother were not actually a real person, he would still be the most important character in some yet-to-be-conceived-story of Chinatown. Would still be real in everyone's minds and hearts, the mythical Asian American man, the ideal mix of assimilated and authentic. Plus, the bonus: a viable romantic lead. Older Brother is the guy who makes every kid in Chinatown want to be better, taller, stronger, faster, more mainstream and somehow less at the same time. Makes every one of you want to be cooler than you're supposed to be, than you're allowed to be. Gives you permission to try.

—For a brief period during Older Brother's ascendancy, all felt right. What was happening was what was meant to happen. The chosen one, the best and brightest and most conventionally-handsome-by-Western-standards, he had worked his way up in the system, had reached his designated station of maximal achievement. All other Asian Men stood in his shadow, feeling anything was possible or, if not anything then at least something. Something was possible. You put your heads on pillows at night and went to sleep dreaming of what it would look like, to be part of the show, lie awake wondering how much higher Older Brother might rise within Black and White. What that would mean for the rest of you.

—And then you woke up one morning and it was over. The dream had ended. Older Brother was no longer Kung Fu Guy. The details secret, the official story that it just didn't work out. The upshot for all of you was: no more Kung Fu Guy. Somehow, the golden era of Older Brother was over, without warning or fanfare or any kind of reason, really. Or at least, no official reason. Unofficially, we understood. There was a ceiling. Always had been, always would be. Even for him. Even for our hero, there were limits to the dream of assimilation, to how far any of you could make your way into the world of Black and White.

It was probably for the best. For him, personally anyway. Older Brother, despite all of his success, never seemed entirely comfortable with his preordained place in the hierarchy, was never totally down with the whole career track. Didn't see himself as a Kung Fu Guy. And he wasn't wrong. His kung fu was too pure, too special to be used the way that everyone knew it would be: flashy, stupid shit, the same moves everyone had seen a million times and yet still wanted him to trot out for every wedding and lunar new year celebration. Better that fame had never happened on him, to preserve his claim for posterity. Better to be a legend than a star.

END OLDER BROTHER AWESOMENESS MONTAGE

*A performer may be
taken in by his own act,
convinced at the moment
that the impression of
reality which he fosters
is the one and only
reality. In such cases we
have a sense in which the
performer comes to be his
own audience; he comes
to be the performer and
observer of the same show.*

Erving Goffman

ACT II

INT. GOLDEN PALACE

SHE'S

the most accomplished young detective
in the history of the department.

HE'S

a third-generation cop who left Wall Street
to honor his father's legacy.

<u>TOGETHER</u>

they head the Impossible Crimes Unit, tasked with
cracking the most unsolvable cases.

When all others have failed, the ICU
is the last hope for <u>justice</u>.

When all others have failed, you call:

<u>BLACK AND WHITE</u>

This is their story.

INT. GOLDEN PALACE CHINESE RESTAURANT—NIGHT

Dead Asian Guy is dead.

                    WHITE LADY COP
          He's dead.

                    BLACK DUDE COP
          Looks that way.

Our heroes regard the prone Asian male body,
partially covered with a sheet.

                    BLACK DUDE COP
          Next of kin?

                    WHITE LADY COP
          Checking.

A crime scene investigator swabs something.
Another measures the radius and dispersal pattern
of a pool of drying blood. A female officer in
uniform (BLACK, 20s, ATTRACTIVE) approaches White
Lady Cop and Black Dude Cop.

                    BLACK DUDE COP
          Whaddya got?

                    ATTRACTIVE OFFICER
          Restaurant worker says the parents
          live nearby. We're hunting down an
          address.

                    WHITE LADY COP
        Good. We'll pay a visit. Might
        have some questions for them.
            (then)
        Anyone else?

                    ATTRACTIVE OFFICER
        A brother.
        Seems to have gone missing.

Black and White exchange a look.

                    BLACK DUDE COP
        This might be a case of—

                    WHITE LADY COP
        The Wong guy.

White: deadpan. Black tries hard but like always,
he breaks first, flashing his trademark smile.
White holds steady a beat longer but then she
breaks, too. It's their show and they have the
comfort of knowing it can't go on without them.
    "Sorry sorry. I'm so sorry," White says, trying
to keep it together. "Can we do that again?"
They've managed to stop laughing when Black's nose
makes a snort and sends them back into another
round of giggles.

BLACK AND WHITE. Two cops, one of each race.
In the opening credits they drive around in a
black-and-white police car, even though they're
detectives. Which doesn't make sense. Often

neither does the plot nor the motivations of the
characters, nor the backstory, nor any of it, if
you think too hard, which means thinking about it
for more than the time spent watching it. But the
template works, and you don't mess with a working
template.

Sometimes there's a Floating Latina. They put her
on marketing materials in select demographically
targeted neighborhoods. Technically on the poster,
but not where your eye lands. She's off to the
side, her head near the edge, smaller than those
of Black and White (and thus, through the magic of
forced perspective, rendered a good ways behind
the two leads). Her pretty face hovering in a sea
of abstract space.

There's a pattern, a form, a certain shape to it
all. The idea that any problem, no matter how
messy and blood-spattered, from EXT. STREET to
INT. OFFICE or INT. CRIME LAB or INT. CHINESE
RESTAURANT, any blight or societal ill, any crime
of hate or intolerance, can be wrapped into the
template. The idea that there are clues, and the
clues can be discovered and understood, at a
reasonable pace, i.e., one major breakthrough or
setback for every commercial break, with each act
a new understanding of the problem. That they, our
heroes, can get to the bottom of things, and in
the end, it's human nature (jealousy and treachery
and, you know, murder). A strangely optimistic
idea. A deeply ingrained hope that they, Black and
White, will be able to face that danger, get a
handle on it. Downtown may be gritty and dark and

full of evil but on some level an unspoken belief, a faith that we live in a manageable world with its own episodic rules and conventions:

Life takes place one hour at a time.

Clues present themselves in order, one at a time.

Two investigators, properly paired, can solve any mystery.

And there's just something about Asians—their faces, their skin color—it just automatically takes you out of this reality. Forces you to step back and say, *Whoa, whoa, what is this? What kind of world are we in? And what are these Asians doing in my cop show?*

There's just something about Asians that makes reality a little too real, overcomplicates the clarity, the duality, the clean elegance of BLACK and WHITE, the proven template and so the decision is made not in some overarching conspiracy to exclude Asians but because it's just easier to keep it how we have it. Two cops roaming the city. The precinct, the car, the bar after work. The decision is made but it's not a decision at all, it's the opposite. It's the way things are. You do the cop show. You get your little check. You wonder: Can you change it? Can you be the one who actually breaks through?

INT. GOLDEN PALACE CHINESE RESTAURANT—TAKE TWO

Dead Asian Guy, still dead.

>   WHITE LADY COP
>   He's dead.

>   BLACK DUDE COP
>   Mmhmm.

>   WHITE LADY COP
>   So we have a body.

>   BLACK DUDE COP
>   We have a body.

CLOSE ON: White Lady Cop.

SARAH GREEN, 31

pretty but tough but emphasis on the pretty. Smart
cookie. Good at her job. Great at her job. Came
from a broken home, worked her way up to become
the most respected detective on the force. Hair
pulled back in a ponytail, suggesting general
competence with the handling of her weapon and
herself and also that she's the kind of gal that
orders draft beer if it's available and is not
averse to glancing at the sports section if it
happens to be lying around. That kind of gal.
Also, pretty. In case that wasn't clear already.
Very very pretty.

                    GREEN
         (gazing at a dead Chinaman)
         What are we looking at?

                 BLACK DUDE COP
         Family drama, probably.
            (pause for effect; chimes
            in the distance, vaguely
            Oriental)
         Some kind of cultural thing.

CLOSE ON: Black Dude Cop.

MILES TURNER, 33.

Tall and built. Really built. Like, if-gray-
T-shirts-hadn't-been-invented-already-they-would-
have-to-be-invented-just-so-Miles-could-wear-the-
shit-out-of-them built. That kind of built.
     Fade tight, edges perfect, skin flawless.
Distractingly handsome. Yale then Goldman then a
hedge fund, on his way to even bigger things when
his father, twenty-seven-year veteran of the NYPD,
was killed in the line of duty. Entered the academy
the day after his dad's funeral, graduated top of
his class. Been on the force ever since—going on
eleven years now, but starting to get antsy.
     Youngest in department history to ever make
detective (recruited by the FBI, as well as several
NYC billionaires to head private security). Cops
don't usually get this famous, but then again
Miles Turner is no ordinary cop. Everyone wants a

piece of him. Currently weighing his options, but
can't bring himself to tell Green yet. They're a
team—and, considering the smoldering looks—maybe
something more?

                    TURNER
               (sexy whisper)
          You hear something?

                              You're off to the
                         side watching all of
                              this. A spectator.

Black and White both turn to look offscreen,
peering into the darkness, their faces lit
perfectly. But there's nothing there. Then:

                    GREEN
          Miles.

                    TURNER
          What?

A sound, from deep background, in the alleyway—
richly audible sound effects.

In the shadows is OLD ASIAN MAN, 70s.

Turner draws his weapon, steady and calm.
Green draws her piece as well, flicks the
safety off, finger on the trigger. She looks
uncharacteristically nervous.

                    TURNER
    Who's there?

                    GREEN
    Hands where we can see them.

                            They're going to
                          shoot him. You have
                            to say something.
                          But how can you? You
                          don't have any lines.

Old Asian Man steps into the light. Turner sees
him just in time.

                    TURNER
        No!

Green lowers her weapon, breathing heavily. Turner
clenches his jaw.

                    GREEN
    Thank you, Miles.

They share a meaningful look—this is the heart of
Black and White, right here, how their partnership
evolves, and of course, all this sexy eye contact.
    In front of them is the person Green almost
shot: Old Asian Man, pushing a cart full of plastic
bottles.
    Turner shifts his weight, nervous.

                         GREEN
             Sir?

                         TURNER
                   (to Green)
             I don't think he understands you.

Turner turns toward Old Asian Man, stoops down a
little.

                    TURNER (CONT'D)
                   (little too loud)
             Do you understand me?

                      OLD ASIAN MAN
                   (without accent)
             Yeah, man. I speak English.

Old Asian Man turns to you and smiles.
   Green laughs. Turner, pissed, looks at the
director.
   The director yells CUT.

Ever since you were a boy, you've dreamt of being Kung Fu Guy.

You're not Kung Fu Guy.

But maybe, just maybe, tomorrow will be the day.

INT. CHINATOWN SRO

Home is a room on the eighth floor of the
Chinatown SRO Apartments. Open a window in the
SRO on a summer night and you can hear at least
five dialects being spoken, the voices bouncing
up and down the central interior courtyard, the
courtyard in reality just a vertical column of
interior-facing windows, also serving as the
community clothes drying space, crisscrossing
lines of kung fu pants for all the Generic Asian
Men, and for the Nameless Asian Women, cheap
knockoff qipaos, slit high up the thigh, or a bit
more modest for Matronly Asian Ladies, terrycloth
bibs for Undernourished Asian Babies, often shown
in montages, and of course don't forget the granny
panties and soiled A-shirts for Old Asian Women
and Old Asian Men, respectively. This interior
space also acting as a conduit for information
via the invisible, complex, and (to an outsider)
incomprehensible inter-window messaging system
for the building, which works in real time and is
lower than the lowest of tech—basically you point
your face in the general direction of the person
you want to communicate with and you yell at them
what you want them to know. Somehow, despite the
cacophony (or because of it) your recipient usually
gets the message.

In the long tradition of immigrants living
above their place of work, the SRO sits on top of
Golden Palace. It goes: ground floor restaurant,
the mezzanine for offices, then seven more floors

of SRO living—fifteen single-room apartments per
floor, a small bathroom with shower and toilet
at the end of the hall. Noises and odors from
the kitchen never stop pushing up from below,
day and night, year-round (even on Thanksgiving
and Christmas), so that when you're sleeping you
are, in a way, still inside the restaurant. You
never really leave Golden Palace, even in your
dreams.

INT. CHINATOWN SRO—STAIRWELL—NIGHT

As you climb the stairs to your room, you pass by
every floor, each one its own ecosystem, its own
set of rules and territories.

The second floor is where your folks live. You
should stop in. It would make her happy. Not that
she would show it. Not that she would smile. More
likely a scowl. You should be a better son. For a
moment. But it won't be a moment. It'll be more. It
will be guilt and that heavy feeling, it will be a
deep sigh, it will be heavy and unspoken and you
don't know if you can do that right now.

The Cheuks live on three. Have lived in the SRO
as long as your parents have. A daughter, who was
smart, but ended up working downstairs, and a son,
Tony Cheuk, who was luckier, was born a boy and
had a chance to move to the city so he did, a good
son who sent money and packages of food; when you
were a kid, a Generic Asian Boy, you'd wander by
their door, hoping to catch him on the right day

and you might get lucky. Tony might give you an almond cookie from Phoenix Bakery or slip you a buck or two just to show off.

There's no fourth floor. Four is very bad. Four sounds like death.

Five is where the Hostess lives (20s, pretty, exotic)—she plays prostitutes so often the women here have shunned her, and the men and older boys hold doors open for her and say how can she be blamed for her beauty, while trying hard not to look too close, her skintight cheongsam hugging every curve. Also on five is the Casino, which is really just a room shared by three Asian Gangsters (late teens to mid-20s, tattoos, their stringy muscles and bony frames not quite filling out their crisp white undershirts; always smoking, even in their sleep).

Sixth floor is where the Monk lives—he hasn't spoken a word in forty years. Older Brother's room was down the hall from the Monk's. He was the only person the Monk would allow, their rooms on opposite ends of the floor.

On seven lives the Emperor. No kid is brave enough to knock on the Emperor's door. Legend has it that, many years ago, the Emperor played, well, an emperor. Ming Dynasty, imperial guards and everything (although by middle school most kids hear the full story, which is that the Emperor was the emperor as in Emperor's Delight, a brand of frozen Oriental Cuisine TV dinners—siu mai and har gow in just two minutes. Steamed buns in three. Just poke holes in the top with your fork, place in the microwave, and in no time you'll be ready to feast like the Emperor himself.

The Emperor's job was to present these plastic trays of steaming delicacies to a family of blond people somewhere in the middle of America, and then bow to them, while off-screen, in the shadows, a gong sounded (and further off-screen, in the mists of history, you could hear the collective weeping of a civilization going back five thousand years). Afterward, the Emperor would get his check and spend it on beer and rice liquor, tipping glass after glass until he was drunk enough to laugh about it, until he was drunk enough that he didn't feel shame or anything else, including his fingers and toes. Not that he had any need to be ashamed around the SRO. He had only admirers, and even today the Emperor has an imperial aura about him from that role, not to mention diminishing but nonnegligible residuals supporting his claim to the throne. A few extra bucks a month goes a long way in this building.

On the eighth floor, you find your mother, standing near your door.

"Have you eaten?"

"What? How did you?"

"Elevator," she says.

"Ma. You know that thing is a death trap. No good thing has ever happened in that elevator."

"You were almost born in there."

"I'm not sure which way that goes."

"You didn't stop by," she says, and instantly your face turns hot.

You hug her and are reminded of how much she has shrunk in recent years, the top of her head maybe reaching your collarbone, if she stands up straight.

"Got some food for you," you say, handing her a plastic bag full of bah-chang.

"This is for me?"

"Yeah."

"You didn't drop it off," she says.

"I figured you'd come and get it eventually."

"Real nice, Willis," she says, but she takes it anyway. You see the scars on her sinewy wrist and forearm—twin belts of raised, darkened skin.

"There are a few different kinds in there. For Dad, too."

She looks in the bag.

"Yeah. The ones I like. With the mushrooms?" She smiles. "Go see your dad later," she says, more a request than a demand.

"How's he doing?"

"Not great. Could use your help."

"He won't talk to me. Not like he used to."

"Not that kind of help. He wants to move the bed over to the wall."

"He doesn't need me for that. The bed's not even—" But then you see the way she is looking at you and you realize: she wouldn't be asking if he could do it.

"Okay," you say. "I'll come down later."

FLASHBACK: YOUR MOTHER

The earliest memories you have of her, she is Young
Beautiful Oriental Woman.

She packs lunches for you, in her off-hours
costume: floral print blouse, polyester bellbottoms. She crouches by the narrow strip that
passes for counter space, assembling a small pian-
tong, a kid's lunch divided into neat compartments:
in the main section, three boiled dumplings filled
with ground pork and bits of ginger and chopped-up
scallions. In the two smaller sections, a dollop
of soft rice with yam, and a handful of slightly
bruised grapes. She presses the lid down tight,
wraps a large rubber band around it for good
measure (you're five, you'll drop the box at
least three times before you eat), and hands it
to you.

You remember a hundred quiet dinners the two of
you had, your father still at work. For dessert,
more grapes or cubed cantaloupe if you're lucky.
If not, a Dixie cup of diluted fruit-punch-
flavored Hi-C. Room temperature but you don't
care. You sip carefully, savoring each taste,
and then when it's almost gone, turn the cup all
the way over until that last stubborn drop makes
its way down the waxy inner surface onto your
tongue. You take the last bite of your dinner and
announce that you're done. I'm full, you say, but
in truth you want a little more and your mother
knows it. She feeds you from her bowl. This close,
you can smell her breath, sharp and almost sweet,

vegetables and garlic. Telling you stories about how she first came to this country. Her dreams of what life would be here.

After dinner, she does the dishes in the communal sink down the hall, wipes them dry, and brings them back in the room, storing them under the table. (In an SRO you think in all three dimensions. A room isn't a layout, a footprint, it's a space, a volume, and when you start to understand that, you can't believe how much volume there is in here. You hang things, and you hang things on those things. You stack and pile and cram, you make use of every available cubic unit of your life, not just a floor plan or a schematic. You find hidden spaces within a hollow object, a hamper or a laundry basket, a box of dried tea leaves, a cookie tin, things inside things inside things.)

After she cleans herself up a bit, she goes downstairs to work at Golden Palace. She works nights, mostly, and the timing is off—her start time an hour or two before your dad gets home. You have a routine: you are allowed to watch television for thirty minutes after Ma leaves, and then you put yourself to bed.

You remember waiting by the front door as she put on her work costume. You remember the moment after she'd gone for the night. When it was quiet. Her emotional energy draining from the room, her protective field slowly dissipating.

FLASHBACK

Your mother studies from a textbook. *How to Make $1,000,000 in Real Estate*. No experience or capital needed, just a few basic principles (location, location, location) and a willingness to work hard.

The Friday nights she doesn't have work are the best. A couple minutes to eight, you look at her and she nods, and you click on the television to the kung fu show. The opening credits get your heart racing. The weary traveler. The white dude that they dressed up to look vaguely Asiatic. But you don't care. You're here for the sound effects. You're here for the martial arts.

The steady rhythm of foot strikes, hand strikes, blows to the torso, blows to the head. Then the music kicks in, jarring dissonant strings, conflict in a minor key. Random gongs.

Push in on our hero.

Push in on his opponent.

The eyes, it's in the eyes.

It's all too much, you can't resist, and you're up, bouncing off the walls of the room, your home, your world, a five-year-old. You are a future Kung Fu Guy in training. Kung Fu Kid.

> KUNG FU KID
> Someday, I'm going to be Bruce Lee.

You repeat it, for effect.

KUNG FU KID

(ahem)
I said, someday, I'm going to be
Bruce Lee.

And then one more time, but still no answer from
your mother, deeply engrossed in her textbook. On-
screen, two fighters crisscrossing six feet above
the ground, somersaults in the air, butterfly
kicks, twisting horizontally, diagonally, three-
sixty, seventy-twenty, ten-eighty. Gravity waiting
patiently for the two black-haired masters to
succumb, not inevitably bound by the rules of
physics like regular mortals, rather by choice,
returning to earth only if and when they feel
like it and even then in their own manner. Blue
sky behind them, the midday sun backlighting the
whole scene in such a way as to wash out
all details—the sweat on their temples, the
features of their chiseled, sinewy torsos—leaving
only the outlines, the stylized and timeless
archetypes of two masters being masterful. Hi-
yah. Kung Fu Kid leaps! Twists! Your leg slicing
through empty space, splitting the world in two.
Wah. Yah. Foom. Doing your own soundtrack. Gearing
up for the big move, full aerial splits, legs
horizontal, toes pointed, your lower body one
straight line, energy shooting from your feet in
both directions . . .

You pulled it off.
First time ever.
. . . Or so you thought, so close to completing

the move but then, as you land, your foot catching
the edge of a plastic tray with your ma's pot of
oolong steeping inside. The tray now tracing out
its own arc through the air, everything in super-
slow-mo, your mother's face somehow remaining calm
through it all, the only flicker in her expression
one of momentary concern, as the pot of scalding
tea nearly hits you on its way down. She catches
it, or almost does, the bulk of the pot landing
on her palm, which must be impervious to pain,
because she doesn't yell or cry out, simply takes
it, absorbing the blow, all of the liquid heat
and force and letting no harm come to your stupid
little head.

Already you can see the red marks forming on her
wrist and forearm, burns that will peel then scar
then darken and firm up into reminders you'll see
years later. After you've gone to bed, you'll hear
her walking up and down the hall, going door to
door asking your neighbors for aloe, but no one
has any or no one has any that they are willing
to part with, so she'll settle for a small glob of
cold toothpaste daubed onto the spot, left there
thick and mint-green. You lie awake, hearing her
come back into the room, bracing yourself for her
wrath or fury or guilt trip, but instead you get
something else entirely. Tenderness. A softening
in her eyes. It's the only thing worse than anger:
advice.

KUNG FU KID
I'm sorry, Ma. I'm really sorry.

                    MA
          (waving you off)
     I don't care about that. Just
     promise me something, okay?

                    KUNG FU KID
     Okay.

                    MA
     Don't grow up to be Kung Fu Guy.

                    KUNG FU KID
     Okay, okay, I promise.
          (then)
     Wait, what?

                    MA
     You heard me. Don't be Kung Fu
     Guy.

                    KUNG FU KID
     Oh. Then what should I be?

                    MA
     Be more.

Lying there in the silence, you try to imagine
what she could possibly mean. Kung Fu Guy is the
pinnacle. How could anyone be more?

INT. CHINATOWN SRO

Most nights in the SRO you go to bed a little
hungry. Which is made worse by having to wait
until one or even two in the morning to take a
shower, the better to avoid the long wait, people
lined up all the way down the hallway and into
the stairwell, holding their toothbrushes, towels
slung over their shoulders, reading the paper,
gossiping, staring at the walls. Nighttime is a
battle against boredom and hunger and heat and
humidity. By midnight, your stomach's making all
kinds of noises, and it becomes a game to imagine
that the various gurgly complaints coming from
your abdomen are actually your internal organs'
way of communicating very specific things to you
("How about a McDonald's Quarter Pounder" or "What
if you cooked your shoe?" or "What if you cooked
your shoe with some garlic and chili sauce?"). A
damp washcloth thrown in the freezer and pulled
out later can be a treat, if someone else doesn't
get to it first.

Once in a long while, late-night fever takes
hold of the building, spreads down one hallway
then up and down the stairwells like wildfire.
Frustration boils into indignation which condenses
into something like, how funny is this shit?
Because at some point, this shit kinda is funny.
Someone says to hell with it and digs out from
the back of the icebox the flank steak they're
supposed to be saving, throws it into a pan, and
fries it up with onions and mushrooms, slices bok
choy and ginger and garlic, sizzle and grease and

the smell floating down and up and all through
the corridor. A teenager turns on some music.
Once that gets going, doors start opening until
they're all open, the whole building buzzing until
sunrise, as if nothing matters because nothing
does matter because the idea was you came here,
your parents and their parents and their parents,
and you always seem to have just arrived and yet
never seem to have actually arrived. You're here,
supposedly, in a new land full of opportunity, but
somehow have gotten trapped in a pretend version
of the old country.

INT. CHINATOWN SRO—EIGHTH FLOOR

You drift off for a while, only realizing you were
asleep at the exact moment you wake, roused by the
familiar and obnoxious sound of idiots trash-
talking one another in various dialects. You open
the door to find them all hanging out, shouting,
playing cards, seems like every male in the
building is there, crowded around your door. The
Generic Asian Men, except up here they've got names:
   The usual suspects. Chen, Lin, Ling, Fong.
   And, it goes without saying Huang, Hung, Chang, Li.
   Lee, Lim, Wu, Wang.
   But also Chu, Yang, Chiu, Tsai, Liao, Fu, Hsieh.
   And even Tang, Mo, Dai, Yan, Zhang, Gong, Gu.
   Not to mention Long, Jiang, Meng, Bai, Wei, Yu.
   Pan, Peng, Ng, Lam, Yip, Sam.
   You poke your head out and they pull you by the
arms into the hallway.

I'm in my underwear, you say, but half of them are, too. By choice.

Someone slaps you on the back. Sup Willis.

Cousin Tsai, man, how you doing? You call him cousin because your moms are cool.

Someone starts talking smack.

Hey hey, everyone listen up.

What?

I'm gonna tell you something.

What?

I'm going to get the part.

You? You?

What? Why not me? I have good hair.

Yeah, but you're short.

We're the same height.

Bullshit.

I bench more than all of you.

You saying we're weak?

No one said that.

So you do think I'm weak.

I didn't say that. You said that.

Said what.

That you're weak.

Say it again.

I didn't say that. But I have no problem saying it to your face. You're weak.

Say it to my face.

I just did.

You're just jealous because my Wing Chun is the best.

No it's not. Anyway, it's not about Wing Chun anymore. They want flashy kicks.

No they don't. They don't even know what Wing
Chun is. They want Taekwondo.

They want Chinese punching and Korean kicks.

They don't know what they want. They want cool
Asian shit.

Finally, agreement all around. Cool Asian shit is
what they want. If you could only figure out what
that means.

You say, what makes any of you think it's going
to be different this time?

What do you mean?

Maybe they make one of us Kung Fu Guy. Maybe a
few good scenes. Maybe a poster, in the back, real
small. And then what?

Silence. They all know you're right.

A beat.

Then Chiu says, man Willis, why you always gotta
be such a downer? The other guys all agree and go
back to playing cards.

INT. CHINATOWN SRO—EIGHTH FLOOR—YOUR ROOM—NIGHT

The main thing about living on eight is that the
shower pan in the bathroom on nine is cracked. It
was cracked when you were a kid, crammed in this
room with your parents, and it's still cracked
now. They've repaired it a half-dozen times in the
past few years but always on the cheap, caulking
it with cheap stuff when what they really need to
do is replace the whole damn thing. Otherwise, it
will just keep cracking over and over again. As,
everyone knows, water hates poor people. Given the

opportunity, water will always find a way to make
poor people miserable, typically at the worst time
possible.

Which, for those living on the eighth floor,
means that every time Old Fong (903) falls asleep
in the shower, or Wang Tai Tai (908), or any one
of the other Old Asian People up there on nine
forgets to shut off the faucet (or can't shut it
tight, on account of rheumatoid arthritis or carpal
tunnel or general infirmity), after about five
minutes, the whole pan floods, which means, for
those of us down here on eight (and parts of seven
on this side of the building), you're sleeping in
half a foot of water for the next several nights.
One time it went all the way down to six and
soaked the little seat cushion that Baby Huang was
sleeping on facedown, and Baby Huang sucked gray
water through nylon for a couple minutes before
her mom woke up to the dripping on her own head,
found her little girl looking a strange color. The
baby lived, but to this day whenever you see her
running down the hall trying to keep up with the
other kids, all you can hear is her sloshy wheeze.
She seems a little slow, although her dad, who
is so nice everyone calls him Nice Guy Huang, is
pretty slow himself (he's never even managed to
become a Generic Asian Man, stuck in nonspeaking),
so who knows, maybe the whole almost drowning in
her own crib didn't affect Baby Huang that much
after all. Not like she was going to the Olympics
anyway. Mostly she's growing up to be a pretty
happy kid, living in this building, in Chinatown,
it's fine. She doesn't know any better.

INT. CHINATOWN SRO—NIGHT

Old Fong fell asleep in the shower again. You
know because the water stains on the ceiling are
starting to darken and get puffy. In about ten
minutes, it'll be raining inside your bedroom.

INT. CHINATOWN SRO—LITTLE LATER

It's raining inside your bedroom. You hope Old Fong
is enjoying his nap.

INT. CHINATOWN SRO—HALLWAY—LATER

Shit. You were wrong. Old Fong didn't fall asleep
in the shower. He died there.
   Someone knocked on the door, telling him his
phone was ringing. Old Fong's son, Young Fong,
calls once a week, to check on his father. Old
Fong usually sits on his bed all day, unwilling
to move. He never misses that call. He'll nibble
on a cracker, or maybe listen to the radio at an
inaudibly low level. Maybe glance at the Taiwanese
newspaper. But mostly, he just stares at his
ancient rotary phone, waiting for it to ring.
   The story, apparently, is that Old Fong waited
all day, and Young Fong didn't call, because he
had to work an extra shift and by the time he
got home, Young Fong figured it was too late. So
he called the next morning, right when Old Fong
had stepped into the shower. Old Fong heard it

and, excited to talk to his son, tried to get out,
slipped and hit his head on the molded soap holder
protruding from the shower wall.

Fatty Choy was apparently the one who found
him. For once, Choy didn't have much to say. He
was quiet for a long time. It took a shot of warm
Christian Brothers and half a can of Coors Light
to get him to stop crying. Then Fatty sat there
stone-faced for another half-hour before explaining
what happened.

Found him on the ground, Fatty says between
slugs of beer. The water pooling. Must have hit the
corner of the sink. Head getting soft like a fruit.

"He kept asking me," he says, "one eye shut.
Asking what happened to his head."

INT. CHINATOWN SRO—LATE NIGHT

Young Fong's here, to collect his father's things.
Everyone's standing around now, trying to figure
out what to say at a moment like this. Wang Tai
Tai opens her mouth to speak, her voice not much
more than a warble.

                    WANG TAI TAI
          You were a good son.

                    YOUNG FONG
          Thank you, Wang Tai Tai.

                    WANG TAI TAI
          You shouldn't feel bad.

YOUNG FONG
I don't. Well, I didn't. But now I
kind of do.

Old Chan shushes Wang Tai Tai, scowls at her. She
scowls back. She's better at scowling than Old
Chan.

You're exhausted, but there's no way you'll be
able to go back to bed. So you bum a cigarette
off of Skinny Lee on the fifth floor, and come out
here to smoke it.

You keep thinking about Old Fong. Not that he
died alone. Not that he died naked, or wet, or with
soap on half his body. That he died waiting for his
son's phone call. That he lived, absolutely sure
that one person in the world would always care,
would always remember to check in on him. And then
in his last moment, he was unsure of whether that
was still true.

Young Fong packs his father's things. A simple
action, done carefully, turns into something more.
He drags an old steamer trunk into the room to
collect the belongings, carefully tucking each
item into place. Smoothing out the threadbare
clothes, as if his father might need them again.
Treating the broken, the inexpensive, the humblest
of possessions with dignity, just as Old Fong had
taught him to do.

Standing there in the hall, you watch through
the doorway, pretending you're not watching through
the doorway. Has he forgotten you're back here, or
does he just not care? The latter, you think. Young

Fong isn't performing for twelve million people a
week, or even twelve, by this point the rest of the
SRO's inhabitants having mostly drifted away. When
he's done, Young Fong inspects the room one last
time, then turns toward his father's empty bed and
lowers his head to say goodbye.

INT. GOLDEN PALACE—AFTER CLOSING

Back inside, the restaurant is closed. The tables
are cleaned, the kitchen is dark.

It's karaoke time at the Golden Palace Chinese
Restaurant.

After all the patrons have finished their
smirky renditions of Marvin Gaye or Stevie Wonder,
tourists tipsy on one too many lychee margarita-
tinis done wailing Whitney or Céline a half-step
flat, after all of that it's the staff's turn at
the microphone. And they don't waste it. Off-duty
busboys warble *corridos* between long pulls from
cans of Tecate, buried in their twang about a
dozen different emotions you forgot you had. But
even they're just the warm-up for the main event.
At the appointed hour, right on time, he appears at
the foot of the stage.

Old Asian Man is on the mic.

Everything goes silent while he adjusts his
glasses, wipes his forehead, takes a sip of water.

"For my friend Fong," he says, and begins singing
John Denver. If you didn't know it already, now you
do: old dudes from rural Taiwan are comfortable

with their karaoke and when they do karaoke for some reason they love no one like they love John Denver.

Maybe it's the dream of the open highway. The romantic myth of the West. A reminder that these funny little Orientals have actually been Americans longer than you have. Know something about this country that you haven't yet figured out. If you don't believe it, go down to your local karaoke bar on a busy night. Wait until the third hour, when the drunk frat boys and gastropub waitresses with headshots are all done with Backstreet Boys and Alicia Keys and locate the slightly older Asian businessman standing patiently in line for his turn, his face warmly rouged on Crown or Japanese lager, and when he steps up and starts slaying "Country Roads," try not to laugh, or wink knowingly or clap a little too hard, because by the time he gets to "West Virginia, mountain mama," you're going to be singing along, and by the time he's done, you might understand why a seventy-seven-year-old guy from a tiny island in the Taiwan Strait who's been in a foreign country for two-thirds of his life can nail a song, note perfect, about wanting to go home.

BLACK AND WHITE
PRODUCTION NOTES

MAKEUP

Taped eyelids
Heavy coloring, emphasizing skin tone

SET DESIGN

Curved eaves
Massive roofs
Pay attention to cornices!
Oriental flourishes and touches
Details are everything

INT. GOLDEN PALACE CHINESE RESTAURANT—NIGHT

Dead Asian Guy is still dead. The Impossible Crimes
Unit is on the case.

                    GREEN
          Let's try to be sensitive here.

                    TURNER
          I'm always sensitive.

Green gives him a look. Then she freezes. She holds
up a finger, silencing Turner.

                    GREEN
          Wait.
               (hears something)
          You hear that?
          Look—

Miles turns to see who Sarah is looking at: an OLD
ASIAN MAN, maybe 70 (although, honestly, if you
said anything between 48 and 88 we'd believe you—
it's hard to tell with Asians. If black don't crack
then yellow just kind of mellows).
     Old Asian Man has an upright bearing, and
despite a softness in and around his midsection,
in his posture and the precision of his movements
there is the sense of an acquired discipline,
something that suggests a deep awareness of his
body and surroundings earned through a lifetime of
focused training.

Green looks at Turner, who now looks less sure
of himself.

                    TURNER
          Go ahead. You talk first.

                    GREEN
          Really? Why?

                    TURNER
          He might be scared of me. A lot of
          older Asians are pretty racist.
               (off her look)
          Sorry. It's true.

Green steps to Old Asian Man.

                    GREEN (CONT'D)
          Hello sir.
               (quick flash of badge)
          Have a second? We'd like to ask
          you a few questions.

Turner has a hand on his weapon. Green looks at
Turner as in: come on dude. Really?
   Turner looks at Green like: what?
   Green looks at Turner like: the gun?
   Turner rolls his eyes like: fine.
   He reluctantly stands down. Clenches his jaw
muscle. It looks awesome when he does this.
People like the clenching, so Turner clenches
a lot.

                    TURNER
        The dead Chinese guy. Did you know
        him?

Old Asian Man doesn't answer, the physiognomy of
his exotic Eastern features, as exacerbated by the
repressive conditioning of his Confucian worldview,
turning his face into an emotionless mask. Foreign,
unknowable even to the trained eye of these
Western detectives, the titular Black and White not
sure what to make of this strange little yellow
man, trying to discern what he's feeling inside.

                 TURNER (CONT'D)
        Hey. You. I'm talking to you.

Turner's playing the tough, so Green can counter
with tact. She softens, her body language, her
tone. The light shifts, and it's tight on Green, her
face center-frame, beauty shot. Her hair shimmers.

                    GREEN
            (sensitive, sincere)
        What my partner's trying to say
        is, did you have any relationship
        with the deceased?

Turner stands down. He clenches again, to show
annoyance. Sexy, sexy annoyance.
    Old Asian Man looks down at his feet. Turner
shifts his weight, nervous.

                    GREEN (CONT'D)
    Sir?

                    TURNER
        (to Green)
    I don't think he understands you.

Turner turns toward Old Asian Man, stoops down a
little.

                    TURNER (CONT'D)
        (little too loud)
    Do you understand her?

                    GREEN
    Sir? Do you understand?
        (to Turner)
    We need a translator.

                    TURNER
    He knows something.

                    GREEN
    Even if he could understand us,
    I'm not sure he'll talk.

                    TURNER
    Maybe he'll be more talkative
    after a ride downtown.

Turner goes for his handcuffs.

                              Watching Old Asian
                                Man there with
                              nothing to do but
                               suffer silently.
                              To give Black and
                              White something
                                to react to.

                         You're so deep in the
                           background, you're
                         almost out of frame.
                          The script doesn't
                           give you anything
                            to say, your only
                           action to sweep the
                         floor. And watch your
                            father get talked
                           to like that. It's
                            his reaction that
                            breaks something
                           inside of you. Or
                            his nonreaction.
                          That this is who he
                           is, Old Asian Man.
                           Nothing more. His
                           acceptance of the
                         role. You have to do
                         something. You step

into focus.

Green turns to look at you. Turner draws his
weapon.

                    TURNER
        Hands where we can see them.

                    GREEN
            (to Turner)
        Will you stop it with the gun?

Turner lowers his firearm slowly. Green approaches,
gets close enough to your face that you can smell
her expensive perfume, see how good her bone
structure is.
    She looks into your eyes.

                    GREEN
        And who are you?
            (slowly, a little loud)
        Sir, please identify yourself.

                GENERIC ASIAN MAN
        I'm no one. But I might be able to
        help you.

Green and Turner look at each other.

                    GREEN
            (to you)
        Excuse us for a minute.

They sidebar.

                    TURNER
        Can we trust him?

                    GREEN
Not sure we have a choice. We need
someone to help us get around
this place.
          (then)
Chinatown is a different world.

                    TURNER
Sarah.

                    GREEN
What?

                    TURNER
You know I was an East Asian
Studies minor—

                    GREEN
At Yale. Yes I know, Miles.
Look, it's cool that you can order
dim sum. But with all due respect
a semester of Cantonese isn't
going to cut it. This is a tight-
knit community. They'll close
ranks, protect their own.
          (then)
If we want the real story, we need
someone on the inside.

Green turns to look at you. It's one of her
signature moves, a piercing, investigatory gaze
at the subject of her attention. This is what

makes her the best cop on the force. Her ability
to see right through to the heart of things.
To make suspects wither, to give witnesses the
courage to tell the truth. Also, her skin tone
is so even. It's like she doesn't have pores
at all.

                    GREEN
              (turns to you)
          You speak English well.

               GENERIC ASIAN MAN
          Thank you.

                   TURNER
          Really well. It's almost like you
          don't have an accent.

Shit. Right. You forgot to do the accent.

                   TURNER
          So can you help us or not?

               GENERIC ASIAN MAN
              (slight accent)
          You want me—to be policeman?

                    GREEN
          We want your help.
              (then)
          The victim's brother, his older
          brother, has gone missing.

This is your chance.

You turn to Green and Turner. You say your line, remembering to do the accent.

> GENERIC ASIAN MAN
> Okay. I help you.

Oriental music plays as we

SMASH TO BLACK

. . . built with an architect, a set designer, and a construction superintendent from the Paramount lot. It featured rickshaw rides for tourists and numerous curio stalls that employed Chinese merchants in costume.

Bonnie Tsui

ACT III
ETHNIC RECURRING

In the morning, you do the cop show.

In the afternoon, you do the cop show.

You get your envelope.

Ninety bucks for being Generic Asian Man.

You train. You stay in shape. You get ready for your next role.

Slowly, you climb the ladder:

Generic Asian Man Number Three.

Generic Asian Man Number Two.

You practice the words you will have to say.

"I did it for my family's honor, officer."

"I have disgraced my family, and now I must pay the price."

"Without face, I have nothing."

"Honor means everything in my culture. You . . . wouldn't understand."

You climb the ladder. Generic Asian Man Number One. You say the words. You train. You stay in shape. You do the cop show. You're close now. Close enough to imagine a different life.

INT. UNMARKED POLICE CAR

Monday morning. A new week. Black and White up front. You in back. Special Guest Star.

                    TURNER
          Let's recap.

                    GREEN
          You don't have to say that.

                    TURNER
Don't have to say what?

                    GREEN
"Let's recap."

                    TURNER
Recapping is important. People
like to be sure of where they are.

                    GREEN
I'm not saying recapping isn't
important. I'm saying you don't
have to say "let's recap."

                    TURNER
What should I say?

                    GREEN
Don't say anything.

                    TURNER
        (to you)
Can you believe this?

No, you think. You can't believe it. How much fun
they're having. How little they care. An Asian
guy is dead, and these two are flirting. It's easy
to squander your lines when you know there will
always be more tomorrow. And the next day, and the
day after that.

                         GREEN
Fine. To recap:
Dead Asian Guy is dead.

                        TURNER
Could be gang-related.

                   SPECIAL GUEST STAR
                     (that's you!)
No. He would never doing a crime.

                         GREEN
Some kind of honor killing then.

                        TURNER
Those are common in Chinatown.

                   SPECIAL GUEST STAR
They are not. None of this sound
like him. Not possible.

                        TURNER
Why? Because you say so?

                   SPECIAL GUEST STAR
If you no need my help, I go back
to restaurant.

                        TURNER
Yeah, why don't you do that.
While you're back there, get me a
lunch special. Number five, beef
broccoli.

GREEN

Miles! What the hell.
(to you)
I'm sorry about that.

Turner looks chastened. Maybe a little embarrassed.
It feels good to have WHITE on your side.

TURNER

(to you)
I don't know why I said that, man.
That's not really who I am.

You pause to consider this. Green snaps you out
of it.

GREEN

Patrol's sweeping the area for
eyewitnesses.

TURNER

All these eyes.
Someone saw something.

GREEN

(to you)
Did he have any enemies? Someone
he had trouble with?

SPECIAL GUEST STAR

No way.

Green gives Turner a meaningful look.

                    TURNER
Are you trying to give me a
meaningful look?

                    GREEN
This is my thing. My thing is this
look.

                    TURNER
You should consider getting
another thing.

                    GREEN
Look who's talking.

                    TURNER
What's that supposed to mean?

                    GREEN
        (sultry)
I'm Miles Turner. My jaw is so
strong and sexy.

            SPECIAL GUEST STAR
Should we focus here? Dead guy
still dead. And now Older Brother
missing.

Uh oh. They both turn to look at you.

                    TURNER
Older Brother? You knew him?

> SPECIAL GUEST STAR
> Everyone knew him. Everyone look
> up to Older Brother. He was number
> one. No one could ever beat him.

Green looks at Turner. Turner looks at Green.
They both look at you. You look at them.
Green looks back at Turner. Turner looks back
at you.

> SPECIAL GUEST STAR
> What?

> TURNER
> What what?

> SPECIAL GUEST STAR
> Why you guys keep giving each
> other looks?

> GREEN
> You said no one could ever beat
> Older Brother.

> SPECIAL GUEST STAR
> Yeah. So?

> TURNER
> Sounds like possible motive to me.

> SPECIAL GUEST STAR
> What motive?

                        GREEN
If someone were to knock him off—

                        TURNER
There's suddenly an opening. An
opportunity.

                    SPECIAL GUEST STAR
For who?

                        GREEN
Every other Asian man in Chinatown.

                    ATTRACTIVE OFFICER
                    (approaches)
Haven't gotten an address yet.

                        GREEN
Well what did you get?

                    ATTRACTIVE OFFICER
                    (hands her slip of paper)
Last known contact was with Ming-
Chen Wu.

Green looks at the name, then looks at you.

                        GREEN
Wu. Any relation?

                    SPECIAL GUEST STAR
We're not all related.

                    TURNER
        Don't lie to us. Do you know him?

                SPECIAL GUEST STAR
        Okay, yes. In this case, I happen
        to know him. But my point still
        stands.

                    TURNER
        Shut up and take us to him.

And then there's the GONG SOUND again. You look
around but can't tell where it's coming from.

INT. GOLDEN PALACE—FRONT OF HOUSE

You enter the restaurant, a step behind Black and
White, your eyes still adjusting to the low light.
Soft music plays. Attractive extras nibble on beef
chow fun. You look around, don't see anyone you
know. Green and Turner look to you. You motion
toward the kitchen.

                SPECIAL GUEST STAR
            In the back.

INT. GOLDEN PALACE—KITCHEN

As you push through the swinging door, a wave of
grease hits first, followed by curse words in seven
different dialects. The staff all turn and look.

Your friends and neighbors, rivals and fellow kung fu students, dressed as prep cooks and dishwashers, looking at you with a mixture of envy and pride. This is the moment you've dreamt of. Coming back here, not as one of them, but as a star. Okay not a star yet. But someone on the rise. An Asian Man who gets to talk.

Old Asian Man is in the corner. You go to him quickly, to have a word in private before Green and Turner catch up.

"Ba," you say, under your breath. He's manning the deep fryer, in a stained undershirt, hair pulled back and tucked under the edges of a white paper hat. As if this were the most natural thing in the world. As if this were all he'd ever done for half a century. As if he hadn't been a dragon, once, not that long ago, hadn't fought epic battles on the streets of Chinatown, and above its rooftops. None of that matters now. None of that counts toward the final tally. Now he's this: a leading man trapped in the body of an extra. He looks tired. He is tired. He spent decades in this place, in the interior of Chinatown, taking the work he could get. Gangster, cook, inscrutable, mystical, nonsensical Oriental.

Now trapped in the back of the house, speaking lines that need subtitles. Thousands of hours of work at something and then in a moment, the work gone. Kung fu master to fry cook, the easiest transition in the world. Change wardrobe, hair, a career forgotten. A lifetime repurposed. A kind of amnesia that he has internalized, a fog of amnesia that hangs over this whole place.

Keng-chhat u bun-te, you say, under your breath, probably mangling it, but he knows what you mean, can decipher your clumsy pronunciation. *The police have questions.* You say it not in Mandarin, but Taiwanese. The family language, the inside language. A secret code.

He acknowledges this with the smallest shift in his eyes.

The kitchen staff run interference, getting in the way of Black and White, giving you just a few extra moments with your dad. He says something you don't quite follow. You hear it, you catch most of the individual words, and yet somehow—you don't understand. This gap, always there. Somehow unbridgeable, whether it's across a wide Pacific gulf of language and culture, or just a simple sentence, father to son, always distance. The texture of everyday actions, simple movements and gestures, is harder than it looks. The great shame of your life that you can't speak his language, not really, not fluently.

"Have you eaten yet, Dad?"

"Yes yes. Are you okay, Willis?"

"Why?"

He flits his eyes toward Green and Turner.

"I'm working with them now. This could be good."

"Happy for you," he says. He looks skeptical. Worried.

Turner and Green, pushing past all the Chinamen, finally reach you. They look suspicious.

GREEN
What were you saying to him?

SPECIAL GUEST STAR
Nothing. I am saying nothing.

TURNER
Didn't look like nothing.

SPECIAL GUEST STAR
Okay, okay. I was asking old man
if knowing something.

Old Asian Man looks at you, a look of disappointment
flickering across his features with each accented
word. You playing this part, talking like a foreigner.
The son who was born here, raised here, a stranger to
his own dad for what. For this. So he could be part
of this, part of the American show, black and white,
no part for yellow. The son who got As in every
subject, including English, now making a living as
Generic Asian Man.
   "I wanted better for you," he says.
   "Dad," you start, but you don't know what to say.
   "Don't say anything? There is nothing left to say."
   "Mom said something earlier. Are you—Ba, are you
okay?"
   He looks down. He's not okay.
   Turner breaks the silence.

TURNER
What's going on here? The real
story.

What does he mean? Your dad—his actual struggles.
It's all you have left. Can you trust him not to

take it away from you? There appears to be more
to Turner and Green than you once thought. But
it's too risky. You've worked too hard to show them
something they might not understand. You need to
keep it together. You can't get fired now. You
make your face into a mask—dead in the eyes. Not
a person. Not a real one anyway. A type. Generic.
It's a form of protection. Keep yourself inside
this costume, this role. You lay it on a little
thicker with the accent, break up your grammar a
bit more.

                    SPECIAL GUEST STAR
          I was just explain to him Older
          Brother is missing. To answer all
          of your questioning so can be
          helpful to detectives in the case.

Turner sees that you're back on script, gets back
into character himself.

                    TURNER
          Is he going to help?

                    SPECIAL GUEST STAR
          He say he will help as much as he
          can.
               (then)
          You know, he used to be someone. A
          teacher. Kung fu.

Turner appraises Old Asian Man.

                    TURNER
So this is him, huh? The master?

              SPECIAL GUEST STAR
Yes. He was my teacher. Taught
everyone in Chinatown. When he
was young man, he was incredible.
He could show you some things.

                    TURNER
Show me some things?
  (laughs)
Okay.

              SPECIAL GUEST STAR
You have muscles, yes, but here,
inside, you are soft. I can see
it. You move slow, like a turtle.

                    TURNER
I'll show you how I move, you
little—

Green pulls Turner aside, out of earshot. Or so
they think.

                    GREEN
Take it easy.

                    TURNER
Why? He started all of this.

                    GREEN
        Yeah, maybe he did. But we
        need him, if we're going to get
        anywhere in Chinatown. Just—be
        nice to the Asian Guy, okay?

There we go. The two words: Asian Guy. Even now,
as Special Guest Star, even here, in your own
neighborhood. Two words that define you, flatten
you, trap you and keep you here. Who you are. All
you are. Your most salient feature, overshadowing
any other feature about you, making irrelevant any
other characteristic. Both necessary and sufficient
for a complete definition of your identity: Asian.
Guy.

                SPECIAL GUEST STAR
        You know, I can hear everything
        you're saying. That's what I am,
        huh? Asian Guy.

Green looks sheepish.

                    GREEN
        I didn't mean—

                SPECIAL GUEST STAR
        Sure you didn't.

                    TURNER
        There are worse things to be
        called.

                    SPECIAL GUEST STAR
Yeah?

                         TURNER
Yeah.
    (then)
Anyway, weren't you the one who
took the role? You want to know the
truth? You did this to yourself.

                    SPECIAL GUEST STAR
I'm choosing this?

                         TURNER
No. But you're going along with
it. Look where we are. Look what
you made yourself into. Working
your way up the system doesn't
mean you beat the system. It
strengthens it. It's what the
system depends on.

                    SPECIAL GUEST STAR
You're part of the system. Your
face is on the poster. Your name
is in the title.

                         TURNER
I am? It says Miles Turner? No, it
doesn't.
It says: BLACK.
    (then)

I'm not a person. I'm a category.
Giving me the lead doesn't make me
any more of a person. If anything,
less. It locks me in. Do you know
where I started? Do you know what
it took? You can't come in here,
five minutes ago, talking about
how hard you have it. If you don't
like it here, go back to China.

With both hands, you push Turner in the chest. He
stumbles back, but catches himself. Wow. His pecs
are like concrete. Round, smooth, pec-shaped slabs
of concrete.

Turner gets up in your face. He's got four inches
and forty pounds on you, all of it muscle.

But your kung fu is solid, and getting better
every day, and for a second, you wonder, what would
Older Brother do? You wonder: could you take him?

He clenches his jaw, puts up his fists, like he
wants to box. You get into a solid fighting stance.
Your left foot tingles, ready for action. It's in
the eyes, you remember your training. And for a
half-second, you see in Turner's eyes the smallest
flicker of doubt.

GREEN
All right break it up.

SPECIAL GUEST STAR
That's right. Listen to your
partner, Miles.

                    TURNER
You really like that, don't you?
When Green sticks up for you.
Feels good to have WHITE on your
side, don't it? Have her approval.

              SPECIAL GUEST STAR
You calling me a model minority?

                    TURNER
You said it, I didn't. Don't you
see? This is how it works. We're
fighting with each other. I don't
want to be doing this any more
than you do. And Green gets to be
the bigger person. Why do you
care what she thinks anyway? You
heard what you are to her: Asian
Guy.

                    GREEN
Feel better? More manly? Hope you
got it all out of your system so
we can get back to work.

Green turns to Old Asian Man, watching this. Unsure
of how to deal with him. He's not a threat, not a
rival, not a subordinate or superior. Definitely
not a potential love interest, no no, come on,
he's an Old Asian Man—now you know, that's how she
thinks of him. And you. And all of you. She stoops
down a couple of inches, talks to him.

GREEN (CONT'D)
Hello sir. Thank you for your help.

Talks to him a little louder than normal, more
than a little, half-shouting almost, as if he's
hard of hearing, while also doing the thing. You
know the thing that people do sometimes with Old
Asian People. The sort of half-assed sign language
except it's not sign language at all, just a
made-up pantomime, as if Old Asians won't otherwise
be able to understand anything you're saying. As
if it takes all of this effort just to get through
to this other consciousness. As if he's an alien.

TURNER
(to Old Asian Man)
Older Brother. When did you last
see him?

Old Asian Man looks at you. As if to ask you: Is
this what you want? For me to answer? You nod. He
hesitates briefly, then answers.

OLD ASIAN MAN
Long time. Been a long time.

GREEN
Weeks?

OLD ASIAN MAN
Longer. Six month, maybe.
(then)
We have argument.

                    TURNER
About what?

                  OLD ASIAN MAN
What else. Money.

                    GREEN
As in, he wanted to borrow money?

                  OLD ASIAN MAN
              (shaking his head)
Not borrow. Give. He want to give
me money. But I don't want it.

Green and Turner look at each other. Then
at you.

                    GREEN
Older Brother shows up, trying to
give away money.

                    TURNER
Laundering?

                    GREEN
Possibly. In any case, sounds like
he had a sudden windfall.

                    TURNER
We follow the money—

                    GREEN
We find our guy.

They're looking at each other now, their faces
having somehow gotten pretty close in the course
of this last exchange. Are they going to kiss?
That would be weird. But it seems like they're
going to kiss. They should just kiss. But then
again, they shouldn't, because if they ever did,
that would be that, no one would care anymore. The
whole point is that they never do. They get their
faces all close and they smolder and they gaze but
they never kiss. Turner finally breaks eye contact
and looks at you.

> TURNER
> (to you)
> So where is it? Where's the money
> in Chinatown?

> GREEN
> This is important. If you know
> something, you have to tell us.

Are you doing the right thing? Something about
this feels wrong.

But this is Black and White. They let you have a
part. You can't stop now.

You look at your dad. He shifts his eyes
away, and you know in that moment that he is
disappointed. But he won't ever say it. You'll
never talk about it again. He's gone, slipped back
into Old Asian Man. He's not going to make the
choice for you. It's your role to play.

                    SPECIAL GUEST STAR
Okay.

                         TURNER
Okay?

                    SPECIAL GUEST STAR
I take you there. I will take you
inside Chinatown.

INT. CHINATOWN GAMBLING DEN

Fatty Choy is working the door. You slap hands, do a one-arm guy hug.

 "Congrats, man," he says under his breath. Turner gives him the once-over, gets up in his personal space.

                    TURNER
          (gruff)
     We need to see your boss.

Fatty Choy's face transforms. One moment he's your boy from the SRO, the next moment he's disappeared, turned into a Lowlife Oriental.

                    LOWLIFE ORIENTAL
     Sorry. Private club. No outsider
     allowed in here.

                    TURNER
     I got a private club for you. It's
     downtown at the precinct. I'll
     book a room and give you a lift—

                    LOWLIFE ORIENTAL
     This is a place of business—

                    GREEN
     Wrong. This is an illegal gambling
     operation.

LOWLIFE ORIENTAL
I don't know anything about no
gambling. I'm just security guard.
You can't arrest me for me just
doing my job.

TURNER
How about I arrest you for an
aggravated assault last week? As
well as public intoxication and a
couple counts of resisting arrest?
How's that sound, Choy? Yeah, we
know who you are.

Turner looks smug as Fatty Choy steps aside. As
you brush past, he mumbles something under his
breath.
    "Willis," he says.
    "Yeah?"
    "Hope you know what you're doing."
    "Me too."
    You make your way through the room hazy with
cigarette smoke, the light click-clack of poker
chips being stacked, shuffled, tossed around.
Sultry Asian Women in high-slit dresses serve
beers and whiskeys to Sleazy Asian Guys in white
T-shirts and slacks. Everyone, men and women,
young and old, looking sketchy, looking like
they'll cut you for cheating or cut you for winning
or just cut you if you look at them wrong. Or at
least that's what they look like to an outsider.
But you know these fools, grew up with most of

them, playing Nintendo or sneaking sips of wine cooler from the fridge in the back of the grocery store on Ninth. Average GPA in this room is probably north of three point seven, and now look at them, pretending to be tough, doing a good job at it, as they do. They're all A students, striving immigrants, still hoping for their shot.

Above it all is the owner of this place, watching the tables from his second-floor office, one eye on the patrons, the other one on his employees.

Turner looks at Green, motions toward the stairs. Green plays it cool, sliding her hand just slightly toward the piece in her waistband as you climb the steps. Turner motions for you to enter first, the two of them falling in behind you.

INT. GAMBLING DEN—BOSS'S OFFICE—CONTINUOUS

As you reach the top of the stairs, the door opens. The Bad Guy of the Week steps out. It's Young Fong. His eyes still red and puffy, his dad not gone even three days and already here's Fong, back to work.

"Hey," you whisper, trying to think of the right thing to say. A kind word. But he plays it straight. Professional. At the moment he's not Fong. He is Chinatown Mini Boss. Medium fish in a small pond. The guy before the guy. Intermediate obstacle. An act two villain who gets you into act three. It's a good gig, even if Fong is

starting to get typecast. Something about how
gentle he is, they love to play off of that,
love how his mild features, his slender build and
slightly pasty complexion, make him the opposite of
Turner, the opposite of masculine, make this Asian
phenotype slightly and inherently creepy to the
Western eye.

                    MINI BOSS
          Detectives.
               (affected, enunciated)
          To what do I owe the pressure?

Turner straight-arms his way into the office.

                    TURNER
          Cut the shit. This isn't a social
          call.

                    MINI BOSS
          Oh. That's too bad. Chinatown has
          much to offer for the adventurous
          traveler.
               (to Turner)
          Those who want to sample its
          exotic flavors.

Fong looks down into the casino at the dozens of
Sultry Asian Women, as if to say, go ahead, choose
one. Turner coughs, uncomfortable, adjusts himself.
Fong gets up and pours himself two generous
fingers of expensive Scotch.

                    MINI BOSS
        I'm sure we can find something to
        your liking.
              (looks at Green)
        Whatever your type may be. We will
        accommodate you.

Fong presses a button on the underside of his
desk, and a moment later a woman steps into the
office. Not just a woman. You don't—you don't know
what to. Uh. Say. Or do. With your arms. Or face.
You're frozen, a schoolboy with a crush. You're an
idiot. Wow.
    She looks at you, and you look at her, and she
looks at you and you can't figure out why she's
looking at you, until you realize you're staring at
her. What—is she? You can't figure it out.
    "Do I know you?" you whisper, but either she
doesn't hear or she ignores the question.

                    TURNER
        Enough bullshit. We're looking for
        someone.

                    MINI BOSS
        You have a warrant? Probable
        cause?

                    GREEN
        We have him.

She points to you. A beat. Silence. Everyone's
looking at you.

                    MINI BOSS
        Oh yeah? And who the hell is he?

                    GREEN
        He's working with us. Impossible
        Crimes Unit.

Turner looks at Green like, what? She looks at you.
You try really hard not to blush, but your legs get
weak and the skin on the back of your neck gets
tingly.

                    GREEN
            (to you)
        It's you, man. Your move.

You clear your throat, trying to sound like you
know what you're doing.

                SPECIAL GUEST STAR
        Older Brother is missing.

Your voice cracks a little. Turner giggles.

                    MINI BOSS
        I heard.

                    GREEN
        We learned that he had a fight
        with his father. He'd recently
        come into some money. Sounds like
        he was looking for a safe place to
        park it.

                    MINI BOSS
And you think I had something to
do with it?

                    TURNER
     (nods toward the casino)
Seems like a pretty good option.

                    MINI BOSS
Yeah. You're right. It does. Except
if you knew anything about Older
Brother, you'd know how stupid
that is.
     (looks at you)
Why didn't you tell them how
stupid that is?

You do your best poker face, but you are bad at
poker. Green reads it on your face.

                    GREEN
What does he mean?

               SPECIAL GUEST STAR
Older Brother didn't care about
money. At all.

                    MINI BOSS
Anyone who knows him would
understand that. He had a plan,
but it had nothing to do with
money.

Turner's ears perk up.

                    TURNER
          What kind of plan? You better
          talk or—

                    MINI BOSS
          Or what? Why should I tell you
          anything?

                    GREEN
          There are enough federal and state
          crimes being committed in this
          building to put you away for a
          very long time.
               (then)
          Unless, of course, you know
          something that could help us.
          Something that might make us
          inclined to go easy.

                    MINI BOSS
          I want immunity.

                    TURNER
          No can do. Not with what we have
          on you.

                    MINI BOSS
          I'm not negotiating.

                    TURNER
          Neither am I.

Turner clenches his jaw. You're not sure if you want to punch his face or caress it.

> GREEN
> We'll put in a good word with the DA's office. Get you the best deal they can manage.

> TURNER
> You might be able to get out to see your children graduate from college.

> MINI BOSS
> Deal, huh? I'm a businessman, detectives, and I know about deals. That is a shit deal.

Fong gives a signal. From downstairs, the sound of a bottle breaking against the craps table. Someone lifts the roulette wheel off its base and flings it across the room like a solid oak Frisbee. It smashes into the bar, spilling tequila and Corona and red wine everywhere. Tables flipping, chips flying, kung fu breaking out all over the place. Shots fired, people diving for cover. Turner and Green draw their weapons and run low toward the window, trying to survey the situation. In the chaos, Fong ducks out a secret exit, leaving behind his mysterious beauty.

"Uh," you say. Real smooth, dumbass. A natural action hero.

"Get low," she says, but it's not in the script and you just stand there, frozen, unsure of what you're supposed to do. She dives, knocking you to the ground just as glass explodes behind you in a spray of bullets, the two of you tumbling to the ground, faces close. It takes you a second to register the fact that she saved your life.

"I'm Karen," she says. Also not in the script.

"Will," you say. "Willis Wu."

"Nice to meet you, Willis Wu."

A henchman appears in the doorway. It's Fatty Choy. You notice him a beat before anyone else and, in one continuous motion, kick up to your feet, execute a front handspring covering three-quarters of the distance, coming in not straight-on but at a right angle from your opponent's nondominant side, kick the gun out of his hand and watch it slide across the floor and stop right at Turner's feet. He turns around, still processing what just happened. You catch your breath. Whoa. You moved fast—faster than anyone in the room. That was some Older Brother-caliber fighting right there. You didn't even know you were capable. Even Sifu might have been impressed.

You pin Fatty to the ground, putting a knee in his back, iron grip on his wrists. Almost like you're a real cop.

"Ow," he groans, quietly. "Dude, give me a break."

Sorry, you say, easing off a little.

"It's cool, Willis. That was some hero shit right there. When did you get so good at kung fu?"

"I don't know," you say. "I guess I've been practicing."

"No shit," he says. "I can tell."

                    SPECIAL GUEST STAR
          Everyone okay?

Green picks herself up, brushes glass off.

                    GREEN
          Nice work.

Turner holsters his weapon, looks rattled.

                    TURNER
              (to you)
          That wasn't proper procedure.

                    GREEN
          Well he saved your ass, Miles.

                    TURNER
          Shit. Where'd Fong go?

Green finds the hidden door, slides it open and closed.

                    GREEN
          Check it out. He got away.

Turner cuffs Fatty, roughs him up a bit, slamming him down into a chair.

                    TURNER
        Talk. Your boss—does he know
        anything about Older Brother? Were
        they working together?

You talk in Fake Chinese to Fatty Choy, and he
pretends to answer in some gibberish he's making
up as he goes along. Then in real Cantonese he
says he's not telling you shit. You turn to Green
and Turner.

                SPECIAL GUEST STAR
        He says he doesn't know anything.

                    WOMAN (O.S.)
        He's lying.

You turn toward the woman, surprised.

                    GREEN
        Wu, this is Detective Karen Lee.
        Although looks like you two have
        already met.

You turn to look at her, trying not to faint. Her
cheekbones. Her earlobes. Her hair! Her hair should
be on a commercial.
    Karen Lee shakes your hand with an iron grip,
flashes a smile, and that's when you realize
where you've seen her before: she's the woman
from the poster. Floating behind Black and
White.

                    SPECIAL GUEST STAR
Thanks.

                          LEE
For what?

                    SPECIAL GUEST STAR
Uh, for saving my life?

                          LEE
I know. I just wanted to hear you
say it. Pretty good footwork back
there, Will. We might be able to
use a guy like you in undercover
vice.

                    SPECIAL GUEST STAR
You mean, like, a full-time role?
Like—

                          LEE
Kung Fu Guy? Maybe. Anything is
possible.

She looks at her hand, which you're still holding.
You let it go. She smiles and leans in. She smells
so good.
    She whispers to you: Let me do the talking. You
nod, unsure why you're going along with her, oh
yeah, you are probably in love with her already,
that's why. She turns back to Green.

                    LEE

He knows something. But he'll
never snitch.

                   TURNER
          (nods, clenches)
Honor is very important to these
people.

                    LEE

Sure. Also, they'll kill his
family.

                   GREEN
          (to Lee)
You learn anything?

                    LEE

You mean before you crashed my
investigation and let the perp get
away? Did I learn anything before
all that shit happened?

                   GREEN

I'm sorry it went down like that,
Karen. But we'll get him.

                   TURNER

Fong's probably halfway to Hong
Kong by now. The money got away.

Lee holds up an Hermès bag.

                    LEE
          Nope. Here's the money.

Turner takes it, opens it, turns it over.

                  TURNER
          Empty.

                    LEE
          Not in the bag. The money is the
          bag.

                  GREEN
             (getting it)
          Counterfeit?

                    LEE
          Fong was running fake luxury
          goods. Chinatown's number one
          export.

                  GREEN
          So what's our next move?

                    LEE
             (turns to you)
          I bet you know where they make
          those bags.

              SPECIAL GUEST STAR
          I do?

                         LEE
            You do.

And then you understand. It's the bridge into the
next scene, how Black and White works, the plot
humming along from clue to clue. You're along for
the ride, part of the story now. Just follow along,
and she'll keep you safe.

                    SPECIAL GUEST STAR
            Right. I do.

                         LEE
            Well, what are we waiting for?
            Let's go.

Karen looks at you as if to say, you and me,
we're in this together. The way she looks at you
makes you melt a little bit and then you realize
your back is wet, and you wonder if maybe you are
actually melting? You touch your shirt, which is
soaked with sweat from the fight, except it's only
on your right side, and you look at your hand and
see it's covered in blood, just like the floor
under you. A lot of blood. Your blood. Which is
when your legs give out, and then you fall down.

                        GREEN
            No!
               (to a patrolman)
            Get a medic here—this, uh, Asian
            Man has been shot.

Turner takes a knee, crouching low to talk to you.

> TURNER
> You helped our investigation.

> SPECIAL GUEST STAR
> Now you nice to me?

> GREEN
> I won't forget this. We won't
> forget it. You have brought honor
> on your family.

> SPECIAL GUEST STAR
> Wait, what?

> TURNER
> You're dying, man.

> SPECIAL GUEST STAR
> What? Already? Are you sure?

> TURNER
> I'm sure.

> SPECIAL GUEST STAR
> I don't understand. How can I be
> dying? I just made it.
> (to Karen)
> I just met you.

Detective Lee looks resigned, but unsurprised.

LEE
I know, Will. I know. I wish it
didn't have to be like this, but
you know how it is. You're an
Asian Man. Your story was great,
while it lasted, but now it's done.
I hope our paths cross again.
Maybe somewhere else.

And you think: no. It won't be somewhere else. It
will be here, again, in Chinatown, next year, same
place. To be yellow in America. A special guest
star, forever the guest.

FADE TO BLACK

*Behind many masks and
many characters, each
performer tends to wear
a single look, a naked
unsocialized look, a look
of concentration, a look
of one who is privately
engaged in a difficult,
treacherous task.*

Erving Goffman

ACT IV
STRIVING IMMIGRANT

Ever since you were a boy, you've dreamt of being Kung Fu Guy.

You are not Kung Fu Guy.

You were close there for a moment. But then you died.

DEATH

When you die, it sucks.

DEATH, PART II

The first thing that happens is you can't work for
forty-five days.

By the coffee and donuts you run into a familiar
face.

"Hey," you say. "Attractive Officer."

"Very Special Guest Star," she says. "Here we
are."

"Surprised to see you here," you say.

"Why would you be surprised?"

"It's *Black and White,*" you say. "Thought you'd
have a bigger part."

"Asian Men aren't the only invisible people
around here, Willis. Look around."

You see what she means. A bunch of Asian dudes
and Black women, nibbling on bear claws, stirring
powdered creamer into paper cups.

"We should do our own thing, someday," she says.
"Black and Yellow."

"You'll be, what? Ex-CIA?"

"Slash supermodel. Slash mother of four," she
says. "Their dad takes care of the kids."

"And I'll be?"

"Whatever you want, man," she says.

"A guy can dream," you say.

"Cheers to that." You touch your small coffee
cups to each other's, a toast to something you both
know will never happen.

DEATH, PART III

Why forty-five days? It's the minimum length
necessary, just long enough for everyone to forget
you existed.

Because even though you all look alike, it's
still weird if you get murdered on Tuesday and by
Thursday you're showing up in the background of a
street scene or as a busboy.

Who knows how they calculate these things but
someone did and figured out the optimal amount
of time. Optimal for them, of course, not for
you. Not for anyone who needs to make a living
as a Delivery Guy, or a Busboy, or an Inscrutable
Background Oriental. Not optimal at all. It feels
like an eternity and no matter how much you might
need the cash, whatever your sob story, sick baby,
hungry kid, Mom needs her medicine, casting won't
even touch you for the mandatory cooling-off
period. Doesn't matter to them. When you're dead,
you are nobody.

Some people think it isn't the worst thing in the world to die. Because if you never die—if you play the same role too long—you start to get confused. Forget who you really are.

Your mother used to die all the time. You always knew when it had happened, because on those days she'd pick you up from school and she'd have taken the pins out of her hair so it fell down to her shoulders and you always thought she looked so glamorous, with her hair like that, with the makeup from work still on. You'd go back to the SRO together and while you washed your face and neck and hands and changed into your sleep clothes she would make you a bowl of fried rice with an egg and a few pickles. Some of the happiest times of your life were when your mother was dead, because you knew it meant she would be home for six weeks, you would have her all to yourself in the afternoons. You would play with a toy or watch television and she would sit next to you, practicing her English while biding her time between lives, always preparing for her next role, however small, for a day, to be someone, if only for a short while.

When she was dead, she got to be your mother.

INT. AMERICAN MOVIES—1950S AND '60S

She'd once dreamed of being more. When she first
started out, as Young Asian Woman. She imagined
a life for herself, full of romance, glamour. One
of the few American stories that had made its way
to the silver screen of Taipei in the '50s, an
afternoon at the cinema with her father and nine
sisters and brothers, sharing one Coke. Being
the eighth of ten, she might get one good sip
before it got taken back by siblings further up
the chain, but that one sip was enough to savor,
sitting up on her heels to get a better view,
holding her father's hand, and watching the perfect
faces, Grace Kelly, Kim Novak, Natalie Wood,
their luminous whiteness shimmering in the cool,
darkened theater.

INT. THE MOVIE VERSION OF HER LIFE—NIGHT

She's in a wine red cheongsam, Mandarin collar,
short sleeves. Gold piping from neck to bottom.
Slits rising up each leg. Nat King Cole on the
jukebox, smoke rising from the tips of cigarettes
held by men sitting in twos and threes, all heads
turning as she descends the stairs.
    And now her costar makes his entrance, Old Asian
Man, but like her, he's young, dashing. He sees her
and is overcome by her beauty.

                    DASHING ASIAN MAN
            I've been looking for you.

PRETTY ASIAN HOSTESS
That so? And now that you've found
me, what do you have to say for
yourself?

He opens his mouth, but the words won't come out.
  She waits in anticipation for him, but there's
no line for him, nothing he can say. No stage
direction, or action lines, or parentheticals
telling them what they're thinking. He looks back
at the door, and at her, trying to remember, but
it's already slipping away. The outside, the world
beyond. A life they could have together, if only
they could figure a way out. Could rent a home or
even, dream of dreams, own one. Find a job, new
costumes, have names other than Asian Woman,
Asian Man.
  Instead, they remain here. In the smoky room,
she in her dress, he in his suit. As we pull
back, we see that this is a golden palace, or
it was, once. When the colors were brighter, the
music swingier. Now it's the Golden Palace Chinese
Restaurant.

INT. GOLDEN PALACE CHINESE RESTAURANT—NIGHT

No less radiant in her cheongsam, she doesn't
descend the stairs. Instead, she stands, dutifully,
at the hostess station, greeting patrons as they
enter.
  He still wears his suit, but the tie is gone,
the top button now open to reveal an undershirt

damp with perspiration, his black slacks now worn
thin in the knees from bending over in the walk-in
freezer, from loading fifty-pound sacks of rice,
from clearing tables of plates with steamed fish,
braised pork, hot and sour soup.

After close, he lingers, waiting to see if she'll
have some tea with him.

> ASIAN MAN/WAITER
> Do you have a name?

> PRETTY ASIAN HOSTESS
> Not really. No.

> ASIAN MAN/WAITER
> Why don't you give yourself one?

> PRETTY ASIAN HOSTESS
> You can do that?

> ASIAN MAN/WAITER
> Why not? It can just be for us.
> Didn't you have a name, that you
> liked? From the movies?

She thinks for a moment, then decides.

> PRETTY ASIAN HOSTESS
> Dorothy. I'll call myself Dorothy.
> And you? What should I call you?

> ASIAN MAN/WAITER
> You can call me Wu. Ming-Chen Wu.

They talk easily, sharing a cigarette, pot after pot of oolong or, her favorite, chrysanthemum, trading backstories.

She'd come from a hard background in the old country, and he smiles in recognition, me too, me too, both of them laughing—Striving Immigrant was the only kind of work they could get. Still, they were appreciative. This was a plot that had a shape to it, something understandable. Tiny, anonymous parts for each of them, an undercurrent of social or political relevance. Hard to see the big picture from their vantage point, but they knew that behind them was a historical backdrop, that they were part of a prestigious project, with the sweep and scope of a grand American narrative. So they do what it takes, make the best of a small role, just to get in.

INT. DOROTHY'S BACKSTORY—HOSPITAL—DAY

She as a nurse's assistant, a yellow girl living in Alabama in 1969. Scale then was a dollar seventy-five an hour, and then a twenty-five-cent raise, making two bucks even, helping to give sponge baths to the older patients, fending off looks and wandering hands. Hey come here, hey you China doll, with the porcelain skin and almond eyes, let me get a look at those slim thighs, and then when the advances were politely yet firmly rebuffed, the quick turn to embarrassed indignation, to entitled anger. To: I think my bedpan needs emptying, to something ugly muttered under the breath.

Home not being much of a safe haven. She'd
stepped off the boat and into the home of her
sister and her sister's husband, a guest (she
thought) whose chores and responsibilities quickly
began to feel more like payment. Her older sister,
Angela, perhaps envious of her younger sister's
looks. How angry Angela had been when she'd
borrowed Angela's sweater, how her brother-in-
law had looked at her in her sweater, how Angela
pretended not to notice. Could draw a line from
that moment to the moment, not three months later,
when she found herself kicked out of the house,
sent packing to live with a different sister in
Ohio. How Angela packed her suitcase for her,
bought a one-way bus ticket to Akron.

(A few months later, Dorothy gets a letter. From
her sister Angela. She opens it, curious. Inside
is a bill, itemized, for the twelve weeks that
Dorothy lived with her sister. Ten cents: bowl of
rice. Fifteen cents: long shower surcharge. Twenty
cents: laundry. Included in the bill is the price
of Dorothy's bus ticket.)

INT. GREYHOUND BUS—AMERICAN BACKROADS—DAY

Dorothy rides the bus through miles of highways,
perhaps nondescript to some, but to her, this is
grandeur. The countryside she pictured, in the
country she long imagined. The panoramic scenery,
the flatness of the landscape, the rivers and
lakes, the gray and blue and silver and pink skies.

It's enough to keep her occupied, to keep her

mind off of the looks from fellow passengers,
from the men at the truck stops where they take
bathroom and meal breaks. Enough to help her
ignore the smell on the bus, four days in early
summer crammed in with fifty-eight strangers. It's
the smell of people, and she can work with that.
She is going north, to Ohio, and she can work with
that, too, moving across the map in her head, like
in a movie, her vector of travel a dashed line
visibly inching across a map of the continent.

To add injury to the insult of having been
kicked out by Angela, Dorothy realizes that her
sister has kept all but one of her books (no doubt
as collateral for the asserted debt). The sole book
now in Dorothy's possession is a copy of Hamilton's
Mythology. A book she has loved since childhood,
when she spied the tattered paperback in a bin in
her local library, passed over by all the other
kids for its ruined state. It says on the back,
published in the U.S.A. She has learned to read
this foreign language from this book, this book
of myths. She loves each of the little chapters,
how they are short, and self-contained, but also
all fit together in a larger universe of gods and
goddesses, spirits, lower and higher, deities of
all types and their seconds, their assistants,
their rivalries and hierarchies, their relative
powers and weaknesses. Their petty squabbles and
sordid doings and secret crushes. Every time she
opens the book, she hopes to turn to a new page,
a new god, a little tiny thing. She likes the minor
gods the best, because they are easier to master,
to learn everything about. She can search out and

soak up all of the other things that other people had written or said about this minor god, and in that way become an authority on such a god. And when she becomes an authority someday, an expert in her own right, she thinks that maybe she might be able to make her own entry in the book. To create a tiny god from scratch. She has not named it yet.

Perhaps the god of bus rides. The god of sponge baths, or maps, or minimum wage. The god of immigrants.

INT. DOROTHY'S FUTURE

Flash-forward. Years later, the book turns up again, in some generational story, of immigrants and assimilation. Dorothy, now Old Asian Woman, will rediscover the book of gods (worn and destroyed by love and overuse, will threaten to fall apart at any moment), will read it to her son in their cramped one-room home. Watch him puzzle over and struggle through each word, his face an oscillating pattern of consternation and joy, the delight from the pronunciation of a word correctly, the pure possibility in his way of reading. The god of first times for everything. The look on his face.

Years after that, Dorothy will get a phone call. Her brother-in-law. Your sister needs help. She will return to Alabama, and find Angela sitting in the dark, in front of a television turned to what appears to be a ten-hour commercial. Angela is wearing a diaper that has not been changed

for a day and a half. She has no food in her
refrigerator and no way to go purchase any.

Dorothy will clean her sister up, carry her to
bed. Make arrangements for her long-term care,
Angela's husband paying for it with their savings.
When the money runs out, and her husband proves
that he's not up to the task, Dorothy will end up
bringing Angela back home with her. She will wipe
and feed her older sister for a year, two days shy
of a year, until Angela expires on a cool autumn
morning.

INT. GOLDEN PALACE CHINESE RESTAURANT

Ming-Chen Wu sits, listening.

                    DOROTHY
          So that's how I ended up here.

She realizes Wu is staring at her. Or gazing, more
like gazing.

                    DOROTHY
          What about you?

Wu snaps out of it, embarrassed, tries to recover.

                    MING-CHEN WU
          What? Oh, sorry, I just—I like
          listening to you talk.

Dorothy suppresses a smile.

                    DOROTHY
     What's your story?

                    MING-CHEN WU
     My story? No, you don't want to
     hear it. Do you?

                    DOROTHY
     Yes I do. I really do.

EXT. MING-CHEN WU'S BACKSTORY

He's a few years older but his path is starkly
different from hers. He was born into Historical
Period Piece, the role given to him was Child
Victim of Oppression.

BEGIN HISTORICAL NEWSREEL MONTAGE:

NEWS READER (V.O.)

On February 28, 1947, the ruling
Nationalist Party, or Kuomintang,
begins what comes to be known
as the 2/28 Incident, a period
of violent suppression of
antigovernment protests. Over
the next several weeks, tens of
thousands of Taiwanese civilians
are killed. *The New York Times*
reports accounts of:

"indiscriminate killing and
looting. For a time everyone seen
on the streets was shot at, homes
were broken into and occupants
killed. In the poorer sections
the streets were said to have
been littered with dead. There
were instances of beheadings and
mutilation of bodies, and women
were raped."

By the evening of March 4, Taiwan
has been placed under martial
law. An uprising of the people
continues for a number of weeks
after, with Taiwanese civilians
controlling much of the island.
Nevertheless, by the end of the
month, the governor general

of Taiwan, Chen Yi, bolstered
by the arrival of troops from
the mainland on March 8, has
regained control. Chen Yi orders
the imprisonment or execution of
the leading organizers he could
identify. His men execute more
than three thousand people.

In 1949, when Chiang Kai-shek
and the Nationalists are finally
and decisively driven from the
mainland by Mao, Chiang and his
loyalists flee to Taiwan, where
they impose martial law again.
This period begins on May 19,
1949. At the time it is lifted
in the summer of 1987, thirty-
eight years and fifty-seven days
later, it is the longest period of
martial law in the world. During
this time, known as the "White
Terror," thousands of Taiwanese
are beaten, killed, or disappeared
by the regime.

At the time of the 2/28 Incident, Young Wu is seven
years old. He sees family members shot in front
of him. He see his home and his town destroyed,
looted, and set on fire. He sees men, and boys,
not much older than he is, at first attempting to
fight, and then attempting to live. He sees his
father running back into his family home, which

is on fire. Count to one hundred, his father says.
And I'll be back here, safe and sound.

INT. GOLDEN PALACE CHINESE RESTAURANT

                    DOROTHY
                (interrupting)
            Why? Why would he do that?

INT. MING-CHEN WU'S BACKSTORY

He waits with his mother and younger siblings, just
babies then, for his father to come out. He counts
to one hundred. He pauses, unsure if he should
keep counting.

   When he reaches ninety-nine, he starts to worry.
At one hundred twenty-one, he starts to cry. At one
hundred eighty-nine, when he is sure his father is
dead, his father emerges from the now completely
blackened front of their small house, carrying a box.

   Young Wu does not know what is in the box, nor
does he ask his father. He guesses his mother
knows, because she looks at the box, and looks at
Young Wu's father, and shakes her head, as if to
say, I can't believe you did that, but also to say,
I understand why you did that.

   Later, Wu will learn what was inside the box:
a piece of paper. The deed to the family plot
of land. This land will be very valuable in the
future. His father risked burning to death for his
children's well-being, the chance at a better life.

But Wu doesn't know this at this moment. What he knows is that the box is valuable, because he just watched his father run into a house on fire for it. Also watching were two Nationalist soldiers, a private and a corporal, who wait until Wu's father emerges, then calmly shoot him through the back, the bullet exiting from his throat. The box, along with the deed, is casually scooped up by the corporal, and the two walk off, leaving Wu's family there, without a father, or a house, or a future.

INT. GOLDEN PALACE CHINESE RESTAURANT

Dorothy places a hand on Wu's shoulder. Lets it rest there.

> DOROTHY
> You never knew him.

> MING-CHEN WU
> Not really, no. There are memories,
> just a couple. Key scenes that
> replay over and over. I was so
> young.
> (then)
> But I was the oldest son. I had to
> do something.

> DOROTHY
> You came here.

Wu takes Dorothy's hand, holds it lightly.

INT. MING-CHEN WU'S BACKSTORY—JOURNEY TO AMERICA

We see Young Wu, moving, in progress, making
his way to the new world. Bright-eyed, full of
hope.

As a young student in Central Taiwan, gazing at
a map of the world in his classroom.

On the map, it is a jeweled blue, sandwiched
between Canada (salmon pink) and Mexico (lime
green). Young Wu dreams of the American air.
Barbecues, baseball on the radio and in the
streets.

In his dreams, he arrives on a bright Monday
morning, the ship pulling into the port, friendly
strangers waving him and the others onto shore.

INT. MING-CHEN WU'S BACKSTORY—THE UNITED STATES

In reality, Young Wu arrives in the dead of night.
He waits in line to have some papers stamped, and
then waits again in an area, sitting with fellow
arrivals from seemingly every country on earth. It
is cold, and except for the buzz of the fluorescent
lights overhead, it is quiet. There is no one
there to greet him. Once he is done here, he will
get on a bus, where he will sit for the next four
days, except for twice-daily stops to eat and use
the restroom, and at the end of four days, he will
arrive in Mississippi, where he will step off of
the bus, in the dead of night, into a swarm of
mosquitoes.

INT. MING-CHEN WU'S BACKSTORY—MISSISSIPPI—1965—DAY

He lives in a house with five other graduate
students, most of them from other countries.
Nakamoto from Japan. Kim and Park from Korea.
Singh, a Punjabi Sikh. And one more: Allen Chen,
also from Taiwan. Young Wu wonders if he and Allen
might be the first two people from Taiwan to ever
live in Mississippi.

He will be paid a modest stipend to teach
students at a university, and to begin graduate
studies, to explore his own field. Young Wu's share
of the rent is fourteen dollars per month. This is
Mississippi, in a college town, in the 1960s. His
graduate student stipend is one hundred dollars a
month. The first time he sees the check, he thinks
there has been a mistake. There has not been a
mistake. Young Wu, for the first and only time in
his life, feels rich.

On top of the hundred dollars per month, he
receives a twenty-five-dollar allowance, once per
quarter, for housing. One semester, he wins an
award for being the best teaching assistant. Half
of the class calls him Chinaman, but mostly they
mean it affectionately. He is an overwhelming
selection for the award. He receives a check for
fifty dollars and a certificate. He makes a frame
for the certificate, and sends the check home, as
he does with almost all of his other checks. In
general, he does well enough that he can afford
to eat at a restaurant, once a month. He does not
like hamburgers at first, but learns to ask for no

mayonnaise or ketchup and eats the meat separately from the bun, lettuce, and tomato.

One day he comes home to find his roommate opening a can of cat food. Young Wu hadn't even known they had a cat in the house. He realizes they don't have a cat, that his friend, Allen Chen, is going to eat the cat food himself.

Young Wu takes the can from Allen, asks him not to do this ever again. Allen points to a whole bag of cat food he has just bought from the market in town. Young Wu says they will find a cat to give it to. He takes Allen to a diner and buys him a hamburger that night, and from then on leaves a couple of dollars on Allen's desk, or in his graduate department mail slot, every week. They look for a cat, together. Allen eventually finds one, and feeds the cat well, for a while.

When the food runs out, the cat keeps coming around, so they feed it leftovers.

All five of Young Wu's housemates are called names. They compare names. Chink, of course, and also slope, jap, nip, gook. Towelhead. Some names are specific, others are quite universal in their function and application. But the one that Wu can never quite get over was the original epithet: Chinaman, the one that seems, in a way, the most harmless, being that in a sense it is literally just a descriptor. China. Man. And yet in that simplicity, in the breadth of its use, it encapsulates so much. This is what you are. Always will be, to me, to us. Not one of us. This other thing.

But mostly the roommates are grad students, and

men, and they do what male grad students do. They
sit at the table, and smoke cigarettes, pooling
money to buy packs.

Young Wu will occasionally take a drag off of
Allen. They smoke, and drink watered-down beer
or cheap whiskey one of them has swiped from a
faculty reception. They laugh and play cards and
compare names they have been called, mostly by
the undergraduates. The faculty are generally
respectful, although for the most part unmistakably
distant. Some are even reasonably warm. A few.
The people in town are the most varied. Many are
polite, if silent. Most are wary, with an edge of
slightly menacing disdain.

One day, Young Wu comes home in an unusually
good mood. Actually humming as he walks into the
house. The day is perfect, jewel blue. Birds sing
along. Young Wu sings himself into the kitchen,
where all of his housemates were sitting at the
table. He stops singing when he sees the looks on
their faces.

It's Allen.

What?

He's in the hospital. Someone beat him unconscious.
Called him a jap.

According to a witness, as the first man hit
Allen in the temple, knocking him to the ground,
they said, "This is for Pearl Harbor."

Young Wu thinks: it could have been him. Nakamoto
says: it should have been him.

All of the housemates realize: it was them. All
of them. That was the point. They are all the
same. All the same to the people who struck Allen

in the head until his eyes swelled shut. All the same as they filled a large sack with batteries and stones, and hit Allen in the stomach with it until blood came up from his throat. Allen was Wu and Park and Kim and Nakamoto, and they were all Allen. Japan, China, Taiwan, Korea, Vietnam. Whatever. Anywhere over there. Slope. Jap. Nip. Chink. Towelhead. Whatever. All of them in the house, after that, they should become closer. But they don't. They don't sit around the table anymore, comparing names. Because now they know what they are. Will always be.

Asian Man.

More and more, they spend time in their rooms studying, or pretending to study. Lying in bed, looking at the ceiling. Singh leaves at the end of the year, transfers to Oregon State. Park and Kim move out, share an apartment on the other side of campus. Young Wu loses track of the others quickly. Eventually, as people do, they all lose track of each other. Except for Allen.

He keeps in touch with Wu, writing letters, which Wu returns, guiltily and belatedly, about one for every three received.

Coming to enjoy, over the years, hearing of Allen's exploits, as he climbs the ladder of academia, then industry, as he turns out to be the best and brightest of them all.

They never catch the three men who beat Allen ninety-five percent of the way to dead. Not that they need to be caught. Everyone knows who did it. Allen goes on to star in *American Dream—Immigrant Success Story*, that rare variation, the mythical promised land, someone leaving Chinatown for the suburbs. Living among the mainstream, which everyone knows means whites.

He goes on to get his doctorate at the Massachusetts Institute of Technology. He gets married, and has two children, a son and a daughter. He suffers headaches for the rest of his life, from the concussion he received in the beating. When he is fifty-one, he is granted a patent, which turns out to have a wide range of industrial applications, opening up whole new possibilities in several fields. The patent is acquired by General Electric for almost three million dollars. It's the first of several dozen patents Allen will go on to file.

Allen, newly rich, with a devoted wife and well-loved and loving children, decides to move out of his house for a while. He thinks about going back to Taiwan, but he had lost his immigration privileges and is afraid he will not be allowed back in if he leaves.

He does not feel at ease in the United States. Taiwan is not home anymore. Increasingly, he finds himself drifting back to Chinatown, where he's treated as a local celebrity. One of us, done good. Made it big. When Allen is fifty-eight years old, he takes half a bottle of sleeping pills and never wakes up. Two years later, Allen's daughter, Christine Chen, graduates from Stanford. Her mother and brother are at the graduation as Christine accepts the departmental citation in physics. She gives a short speech, in which she thanks her mother and her father. Her mother

cries, and her brother claps. They all go out to
dinner afterward. Two weeks after graduation,
Christine is filling her car with gas at a rest
stop off of the I-5. Someone yells out the window
of a car moving at close to forty miles per hour
that she should go back to where she came from,
and throws a half-full beer bottle at her head. She
is taken to the emergency room, where her scalp
is sewn up with eleven stitches. She goes on to
be a lead researcher at CERN, but like her father,
suffers headaches for the rest of her life. She
never visits Chinatown anymore.

Young Wu finishes his two years at Mississippi
with a 3.94 grade point average. When he graduates,
he is accepted in a doctoral program at UCLA.

Wu passes his qualifying exams at the end of
his first year. Halfway through his second year,
his mother falls ill, requiring him to drop out
to earn money. He looks for work in his field.
In other fields. Willing to apply his skills. But
there are few takers, despite his grades. After one
particularly bad interview, the recruiter offers
some unsolicited advice.

"No one really wants to hire you," he says. "It's
your accent."

"I don't have an accent," Wu replies.

"Exactly. It's weird."

So Wu learns to do an accent, and then gets
a job, the only one he can, as Young Asian Man,
at Fortune Palace, a restaurant. Washing dishes,
busing tables. In Chinatown.

He does the accent, learns how the place works.

It is not who he is, but he learns how to be Young Asian Man, gets good at it.

EXT. DOROTHY'S BACKSTORY

She moves to Chinatown from Ohio, packs her one blue suitcase. She brings six blouses, four pairs of polyester pants. She brings a picture of her mother and father, standing up straight and about a foot apart, not touching, taken on the street in Taipei where they first met. They are both looking right into the camera.

She brings seven pairs of underwear, two pairs of shoes. She brings an anxious disposition. She brings a rowdy, somewhat unexpected laugh, the kind that erupts suddenly in a noisy party and then just as quickly disappears. She brings a memory of her mother dying in her bed at home, surrounded by her ten children, wondering aloud why, why, the question, undisguised. Why? Dorothy, throughout her life, will wonder now and then if that memory is trustworthy, or her own thoughts bleeding, over time, seepage from the frame into the picture.

She brings incense, and a shrine to her ancestors, and a smaller one for a particular, minor deity. The minor god of immigration and prosperity in real estate transactions. Which started out, a long time ago, as the greater spirit of irrigation and good fortune in agriculture. This is a deity who understands, above all: location, location, location.

To pray to the minor god, you close your eyes and you imagine a home for you and your family, with four bedrooms and two and a half baths, and you open your eyes and see yourself in southern California, and then you are.

But despite her prayers, people do not want to sell Dorothy and Wu a house. And that's okay, because they can't afford one. But people also do not want to rent them an apartment. Which would also be understandable, as Dorothy and Wu have a meager income, except that their income isn't the reason no one will rent to them. The reason no one will rent to them is the color of their skin, and although technically at this point in the story of America this reason for not renting to someone is illegal, the reality is, no one cares. The minor god of immigration has gotten Dorothy this far, but the real estate spirits have failed her. She and Wu rent in the only place they can go, which has the benefit of being a place they can afford. The Chinatown SRO.

They take the biggest room they can find, on the best floor (the eighth), in a room that is twelve feet by ten (half again as large as the standard ten by eight), their double incomes, as Young Asian Man and Pretty Asian Hostess affording them a life of relative comfort, which is not saying much. But they can eat fish with most meals, and meat once a week, and they don't have to buy broken rice like many who live on the floors below.

They go downstairs together, working nights in the restaurant. She in the front of the house, he in the back. In her new job, she is scanned and

studied, admired and assessed, pinched, grabbed,
slapped, and, worst of all, caressed. The caressers
fancy themselves to be gentlemen. They imagine
that Dorothy returns their affections, plays coy
or demure or even outraged, as part of the role.
These gentlemen don't go for the quick palmful
of buttock or breast, the momentary violation.
Instead, they imagine a world where they could
keep her, in some small apartment, and visit their
little China doll.

Wu watches this, and bites his tongue. This is
not the story. He is not a kung fu master yet, not
supposed to defend her by taking out all these
suckers with lightning strikes from his left foot.
It takes great restraint, and constant reassurance
from Dorothy, that he's doing the right thing, that
they must do this to survive. Pretty Asian Hostess
is what pays the bills for them, and he knows
it, and that makes it even worse. In this place,
Golden Palace, Dorothy is almost a star, the light
hits her just so, focusing on the curve of her hip,
the way the qipao fits her. This is what she is,
and all she is, good for some eye candy while the
businessmen talk to the crime bosses, the seedy
underworld scene plays out. Sometimes she lives.
Many nights, she dies. Opium, maybe, or a revenge
killing. Some spurned lover. Or caught in the cross
fire.

Sometimes she gets to weep before she dies, and
on those nights, Wu will stop what he's doing,
stand in the background, and watch her work. Watch
everyone else watching her, too. Transfixed. And
he'll know she's destined for more. She weeps,

then she dies, then they go upstairs and wash up,
celebrate by sharing a bowl of noodles with a few
preserved radishes on top.

On off days, they venture out into EXT.
CHINATOWN, not able to make it very far before
they reach the end of the block, the area where
the scenery ends. But it's enough, to get some
fresh air, to see real daylight, to hear sounds
without a soundtrack.

Dorothy tends toward those polyester bellbottoms
and floral print blouses, with long, low, pointy
collars. She pushes her midnight black hair
back out of her face with a headband. She tries
on looks, American woman looks, and with her
fair complexion, she gets a kind of soft pass—
begrudging admiration from the women, straight-up
ogling from the men.

She isn't often called chink, although sometimes
when she speaks, people have a hard time
understanding her, or at least they pretend to
have a hard time.

Young Wu has a harder time fitting in. Wears
pants an inch too short. Short-sleeved shirts boxy
and too big for his wiry frame. They split a Coke,
just like Dorothy used to do with her whole family,
and she drinks too much and gets a stomachache,
and he holds her hand and lightly rubs her belly.

Young Wu turns to Dorothy and stops.

What is it?

We're going to get out of here.

At the end of the night, Young Wu has a look in
his eye, and this is the first time Dorothy has
ever seen that look on Young Wu's face. The first

time Dorothy had ever seen that look on anyone's
face. It scares her a little. But it is also when
she finally falls for him.

                    MING-CHEN WU
          This is how we met. And fell in
          love.

                    DOROTHY
          In this place? This is no place
          for a romance. This is a place for
          the police to find dead bodies.
          This is a place where day and
          night are interchangeable, where
          we don't know who we are allowed
          to be, from one day to the next.
          How do we have a love story in a
          place like this?

                    MING-CHEN WU
          It's true. We don't choose our
          circumstances. We will have to
          fall in love when we can. Stolen
          moments. Between jobs, between
          scenes. Not a love story. But our
          story.

   They're married in the restaurant, a small
impromptu gathering of the waitstaff and cooks and
busboys.
   They luck out—two rock crabs get sent back
to the kitchen, and a lobster comes back almost
untouched, and they use every part of the

crustaceans, frying up rice with the eggs, dicing up meat to eat with noodles. Someone turns on the radio. There's eating and dancing, and it's hot as hell, everyone sweating through their costumes, but no one cares tonight.

In the swirl of bodies, Wu takes Dorothy's hand, holds it lightly, whispers to her. *Not a love story,* he says. *Not our story. Just us together. More than enough.* She kisses him. A cheer goes up. Some large bottles of Tsingtao are procured, and it's a good time until they remember where they are. Who they are. The boss comes back to the kitchen and tells everyone to get back to work. Dorothy and Wu take a moment to collect themselves, and with heavy heads and limbs and full stomachs and hearts, put their Asian costumes back on.

GENERIC ASIAN KID

And then you arrive on the scene, Baby Willis.
A little tiny Kung Fu Boy. And for a moment the
backstories and fragments and scenes filled with
background players and nonspeaking parts, it all
makes a kind of sense, all of it leading to this.
A family. They bring you home from the hospital,
at which point everything speeds up. It's a montage
of first moments, all of the major and minor
milestones: first step, first word, first time
sleeping through the night. There are a few years
in a family when, if everything goes right, the
parents aren't alone anymore, they've been raising
their own companion, the kid who's going to
make them less alone in the world and for those
years they are less alone. It's a blur—dense,
raucous, exhausting—feelings and thoughts all
jumbled together into days and semesters, routines
and first times, rolling along, rambling along,
summer nights with all the windows open, lying on
top of the covers, and darkening autumn mornings
when no one wants to get out of bed, getting
ready, getting better at things, wins and losses
and days when it doesn't go anyone's way at all,
and then, just as chaos begins to take some kind
of shape, present itself not as a random series of
emergencies and things you could have done better,
the calendar, the months and years and year after
year, stacked up in a messy pile starts to make
sense, the sweetness of it all, right at that
moment, the first times start turning into last
times, as in, last first day of school, last time

he crawls into bed with us, last time you'll all sleep together like this, the three of you. There are a few years when you make almost all of your important memories. And then you spend the next few decades reliving them.

GENERIC ASIAN FAMILY

You have done this before, all of it. Have done
your best to become Americans. Watched the
shows, listened to the tapes, eliminated your
accents. Dressed right, did your hair, took golf
lessons. Encouraged English at home, even. You did
everything that was asked of you and more.

Your parents, they work. For the pleasure of
strangers, losing themselves in their various
guises. Saying the words, hitting the marks,
standing near the good light.

From the background, you watch.

At night, your mother puts on the costume.

At night, your father studies kung fu.

They weep, they die. They get by.

Finally, after years, he perfects it. He emerges
one day as a kung fu master.

He gets work as Sifu. He's in high demand.

You celebrate by frying up a steak, the three
of you eating happily and washing the greasy meat
down with a two-liter of Coke. A toast: to not
being other people anymore. Your parents make
plans to move from the SRO. Everything is going
well. Until it's not.

Until your father realizes that, despite it all,
the bigger check, the honorable title, the status
in the show, who he is. Fu Manchu. Yellow Man.
Everything has changed, nothing has changed.

Yes, yes, your kung fu is perfect. Immaculate,
pristine, Platonically Ideal Kung Fu from the
highest plane of martial arts. But, and we hate to
ask this—can you still do the accent?

They ask him to put on silly hats. To cook chop
suey, jump-kick vegetables into a thousand pieces.
He hears a gong wherever he goes.

He is told: you are a legend.

You see where this is all headed, but it's too
late. You can't control it. Neither can he.

Your mother weeps, and dies. Weeps and dies.
Weeps and doesn't die. Just weeps. Because now,
your father is no longer a person, no longer a
human. Just some mystical Eastern force, some
Wizened Chinaman. Her husband is gone, Wu is
gone, even Young Asian Man is gone. They took him
away from her. He is lost now, in his work, in
who they made him. Distant. Cold, perfectionist.
Inscrutable. No descriptors, anymore, no age or
build, just a role, a name, a shell where he used
to be. His features taken away and replaced by
archetypes, even his face hollowing out.

This is how he became Sifu. This is how she lost
her husband. How you lost your dad.

He comes in and out of the room, odd hours, waking
you and your mother up to rant about this or
that, to tell you his plans, how he will show them
one day, to imagine a world in which his son can
grow up proud to be in this family. He does this
regularly if infrequently, then sporadically, then
not at all. You get news of him from others in
the building, hear rumors. He's taken to drinking,
breaking props. They put him in epics, and he
disappears for long stretches, just rumbling drums
and violent strings and always gongs, always always
gongs. They push in on his eyes, the dead eyes,

they've turned him into what they wanted, what he
was destined for all along, a cheaper version of
Bruce Lee. You grow up like this, in Chinatown,
your dad no longer your dad. You can hear them
talking at night, about how to get out, about the
dream of getting out, about never getting out.

                    YOUNG ASIAN MAN
            What happened? What have they
            done? They've trapped us.

                    YOUNG ASIAN WOMAN
            Or maybe we did it to ourselves.

                    YOUNG ASIAN MAN
            Were we always this? Wasn't there
            more?

                    YOUNG ASIAN WOMAN
            There was. There can be more.

You hear them at night and you think: someday,
you'll get out.

162

EXT. THE ALLEY BEHIND THE RESTAURANT—PRESENT DAY

First drag's the best drag. Second drag you remember
you hate smoking. You hold the cigarette away from
your body, watch the lonely ribbon drift up toward
the billboard, thirty feet high in the sky:

MILES TURNER   SARAH GREEN

BLACK AND WHITE

their perfect, huge faces, looking down on you.
Even out here, the light hits their faces just
right. Wherever they go that's where they're meant
to be, the center of things always white and black
and black and white. Even in the picture, the
tension is unbearable, some spot halfway between
their two noses the romantic center of gravity, the
two of them facing each other, in profile. Both of
them with such luscious lips. Are those their real
lips? They can't be. You take your thumb and index
finger to your own lips, checking to see how meaty
they are. How do you get lips like that? Lips that
look permanently ready to be kissed, a perpetual
state of plumpness. Supple. Pouty and tough. Those
are some sexy cops with sexy lips. You wish your
face was more—more, something. You don't know what.
Maybe not more. Less. Less flat. Less delicate.
More rugged. Your jawline more defined. This face
that feels like a mask, that has never felt quite
right on you. That reminds you, at odd times, and
often after two to four drinks, that you're Asian.

You are Asian! Your brain forgets sometimes. But
then your face reminds you.

The door swings out, startling you. It's her.
Karen Lee.

"Easy there," she says. "How's death?"

"Are you talking to me?" you ask her.

She looks around, as in, who else, dude?

"Sorry. I'm not used to, uh, women like you
talking to guys like, uh . . ."

"Women like me?"

"Women with options."

She laughs. Studies you for a moment. "You're not
really smoking, are you?"

You look at your cigarette. "No."

"Then why are you holding that?"

"I don't know. Goes with the outfit, I guess."
You drop the cigarette, crush it out with your
shoe.

"So. How are you?"

Whoa, you think. Is she messing with you? She's
messing with you. She has to be messing with you.
A woman like this is not going to be interested in
a Dead Not Quite Kung Fu Guy. A Generic Asian Man.
If there's one thing that you have to remember,
it's that. Sure, they'll talk to you. Be your
friend. But deep down, she doesn't think of you
like that—

"Hey, Will, you still there? Lost in your
internal monologue?"

"Sorry. I guess so."

"It's nice out, isn't it?"

"Yeah."

"Where are you from?"

"I'm from here. Chinatown. What about you?"

She flashes her eyes at you, and you almost die all over again. "Where do you think I'm from?" she asks.

"You want me to guess?

"I want to know your impression of me."

"Okay," you say. "I'll give it a shot: you went to a good-to-very-good liberal arts college in the Midwest. No—back east. You know how to ride a horse, drive stick, use chopsticks. You did a semester abroad in Osaka, yeah? Or Kyoto maybe. Solid grades. You have an accounting degree to fall back on if your dreams don't work out."

"So far so good, except it was Taipei, not Osaka, history, not accounting, and I was dean's list all four years, and to be honest, I'm not sure what my dream is yet—it might be grad school—so I don't think I'll be crushed if, as you put it, it doesn't pan out for me."

"But that's the thing, Karen. For you, it always does. One way or another. Pretty Girl is never not going to be in demand. Kind of how it goes. Things work out pretty good for your kind. White People: Pretty Much Good, Pretty Much Always. Didn't they teach that in history?"

"I'm not White."

"White-ish. Close enough."

"Yeah. That's why I play Ethnically Ambiguous Woman Number One."

"You may have a point. So what . . . are you?"

"What am I? Nice, Willis."

"You know what I mean. Lee can be, you know, like Sara Lee, or General Lee. But it's actually, like, Lee. As in, Lee?"

"Lee, as in my paternal grandfather was from Taichung. He moved to the States and lived with us after my grandmother died."

"You're a quarter Taiwanese?"

"If you want to quantify it that way."

"Wow. Just—wow."

"What did you think I was?"

"I don't know. I thought maybe you were part Latina? Or maybe just came back from Hawaii and had a nice tan? Do you speak?"

"*E-hiau kong Tai-oan-oe.*"

"From your accent I can tell you speak better than I do."

"Do you need a moment?"

"This is very confusing for me."

"If you think it's confusing for you, imagine how I feel."

"Seems like it's worked out pretty well for you."

"I'm sure it seems that way."

"You're like a magical creature. A chameleon."

"Able to pass in any situation as may be required," she says. "I get it all. Brazilian, Filipina, Mediterranean, Eurasian. Or just a really tan White girl with exotic-looking eyes. Everywhere I go, people think I'm one of them. They want to claim me for their tribe."

"Must be amazing."

"Yeah, I mean, I can be objectified by men of all races."

"But you said it yourself. You can pass for anything."

"Seems like it'd be easier to be one thing."

"I'm one thing. An Asian Man. And that's all I am. Trust me, it's better to be you than me."

"Oh, boo hoo, I'm a poor helpless Asian Man. It's so terrible being me."

"I have to talk with an accent because no one can process what the hell to do with me. I've got the consciousness of a contemporary American. And the face of a Chinese farmer of five thousand years ago. Asian Man. It's a fact. Look it up. No one likes us."

"Not with that attitude they won't. And by the way, I think I might like you. Maybe. A little."

Wait, what?

LOVE STORY FOR A GENERIC ASIAN MAN???

No way.

LOVE STORY FOR A GENERIC ASIAN MAN???

For real?

LOVE STORY FOR A GENERIC ASIAN MAN???

They're rare, for your kind, but if you're lucky, in a lifetime, you might get one good one. Make it count.

LOVE STORY

You and Karen. The scene is set. Take your places.
She's a tourist, you're a Delivery Guy. You can't
stop looking at her.

BEGIN ROMANTIC MONTAGE

> KAREN
> Oh.
> Are we starting already?

> SPECIAL GUEST STAR
> And for some inexplicable reason,
> she likes you.

> KAREN
> I guess we're starting.
> Why inexplicable?

> SPECIAL GUEST STAR
> Because look at you.
> And look at me.

> KAREN
> Why are we talking like this?

"Sorry," you say. "Force of habit."

"I don't want to practice dating, Will. I want to
actually date."

"How do we do that?"

"You don't know how to date?"

"Not really," you say, looking down.

"Oh. Oh! I thought you were kidding," she says, realizing you are not. "Why don't we start with coffee?"

"I like coffee."

At coffee you ask her questions. What are her hopes, her fears? Where does she see herself in five years? She says those are bad questions. Those are questions if she were interviewing for a position at a law firm, not questions to ask on a date. You say right, right, as if you knew that, and then it is quiet for a second and she starts laughing and your face goes flush and you feel like you might have to run out of the coffee place but instead you start laughing at yourself and it feels so good. To have no idea what you are supposed to do or say and to be sitting across from this person who has just taken your hand and squeezed it then let go right away and then you're walking EXT. BOARDWALK—NIGHT, under the moonlight and she says, hey, how did we get here? You say moonlit strolls along the water are supposed to be romantic and she says this isn't a place, it's an idea, a generic romantic setting and you say well they don't call me Generic Asian Man for nothing and you laugh at yourself and this time it's easier and she laughs, too. This time instead of her making you laugh, you made her laugh and that feels good, making this person laugh, and you tell her that. She says she always thought you were funny. She'd worked with you before, and in the background you were always making cracks, whispering stuff to Fatty Choy or one of

the other guys, little jokes under your breath,
pretending that you were just trying to deliver
a takeout order of Fried Rice Combo but then you
accidentally witnessed several murders and that
BLACK AND WHITE was really, at its heart, a show
about the dangers of eating too much Chinese food. ✓

You really noticed me? You want to ask her but
you don't. You just let that fact sit with you—
Karen Lee was aware of your existence before the
two of you met. She saw you back there, not in the
light, even when you weren't able to see yourself,
and that fact changes everything. Now you're INT.
CHINATOWN, sharing a bowl of tsuabing shaved ice
with red bean and condensed milk and you're asking
her questions about herself. You find out she has
four younger brothers, the youngest of whom is in
middle school. Her dad died when she was fifteen
and her mom remarried. You like looking at her,
it's true, seeing in her face, her features, little
habits that you recognize, a Chinatown face, and
also things that you don't, some threshold ratio of
familiarity and difference, of comfort and newness,
extending not just to the way she talks, the tones
and rhythms of speech, but also thought, to the
way she sees the world—from the background, from
the margin. She may look like a future leading
lady but she has the clear-eyed pragmatism of
someone who started in bit parts. She takes care
of people—her brothers, her mother—and you start
to imagine ways that you could take care of her,
care for the one who is always caring for others.
You like how she is self-aware without being overly
self-conscious, how she says what she means and

does what she believes in. Your whole life you've wanted to be Kung Fu Guy, to be something you are not, and here is this person who is whatever she is at all times.

More coffee, more cold desserts. Talking. Some kissing happens. More talking. You play games. Would You Rather. Would you rather: be Handsome Dead Asian with no lines or Silly Oriental who says silly things? You do voices, slip into roles you've both done, share the dumbest things you've ever had to say at work. More tea, more eating of fried things, things on sticks, and laughing and taking on goofy roles. You want to tell her how you feel. You rehearse what you're going to say, imagine yourself in profile, dewy and tender-eyed. She notices you rehearsing.

"Will? What are you doing?"

"Being in love with you."

"No, you're not. You're falling in love."

"Same thing."

"Not the same thing," she says. "Falling in love is a story."

She says that telling a love story is something one person does. Being in love takes both of them. Putting her on a pedestal is just a different way of being alone.

You try not to ruin this. She doesn't let you ruin it. It's going well. It keeps going well until the point where it normally stops going well and seems like it's going to start going less well, but then it gets to that point and it doesn't stop going well.

Karen sees you, talking to your mother. She

approaches, smiling, nervous, sweet. A feeling
rises up in you, a taste in your mouth, metallic,
like fear. Karen and Old Asian Woman, meeting,
in conversation. You can't imagine it. You can't
imagine it so you can't let it happen. How do you
stop this? Run away? Tackle her? Tackle your mom?
But none of that's necessary. All that happens is
you do a thing, small, a turn of your head.

"Oh," she says. "You don't want me to meet her."

"I do, it's just," you say. "She's not the
easiest—"

"It's fine, Will. I get it." And she does. Karen
doesn't let you ruin things. She understands your
anxiety. She waits until you're ready for them to
meet.

When you do introduce them, your mother doesn't
say much. She smiles warmly, shakes her hand.
Speaks some Taiwanese to her. Karen answers back.
In Taiwanese. Karen says something about you that
you don't quite understand. Your mom laughs. They
both turn and look at you, smiling. What the hell
is happening? This is not the way things are
supposed to go. This is supposed to be when things
fall apart but instead they are doing the opposite.

And then you stop being dead.

END ROMANTIC MONTAGE

BLACK AND WHITE

POST-DEATH

NOTICE OF REINSTATEMENT

RE: WILLIS WU

This is to confirm completion of the mandatory forty-five (45) day silent period following your most recent death event. You may now resume activities. Please note that by re-entering the system, you hereby acknowledge and agree to waive any and all status or other accumulated benefits you may have accrued pre-death. No continuity with any previous role will be recognized.

—CENTRAL CASTING

You share the news with Karen. This should be a good thing. For you to be back at work, with more purpose, more money to spend on dates. To save toward a future. You celebrate together over beer and noodles.

You start working again. Same shit jobs, but now you have confidence. Now you have Karen. You start doing better. Still bit parts, but the bits are slightly larger.

You climb the ladder. Again.

Generic Asian Man Number Three, Two, One.

Karen's career continues on its ascent as well—a higher, faster arc than yours. That doesn't bother you. You're happy for her. You are. You know she's destined for bigger things than you. Dating someone more successful than you comes with the territory of being who you are—there are more roles for Karen. Apples and oranges. Doesn't bother you in the least.

You see each other less. Twice a week becomes once, becomes once every other week. You talk but you don't.

"Hey."

"Hey."

"Where have you been?"

"Working."

"Okay."

"A lot."

"Do they not give you breaks?"

"I have to focus on my career."

You do. And Karen supports you. Her support gives you even more confidence which leads to even more work which leads to more confidence. No more

Generic—now you're a guest star again. There's
something about you that's different. They can see
it, whoever they are that make these decisions.
You've got that intangible something now. That's
what they tell you. Guest star, guest star,
guest star, and then next thing you know, you're
recurring. You're on the verge of something, a big
break. You can feel it. And then it happens for
you. A meeting with the director.

He tells you: All these years. Ever since you
were a boy. What have you dreamed of? He tells
you it's right there. You're so close. Just keep
working. Any day now.

You can't believe the news. Kung Fu Guy. Any day
now.

The plan is to share the news with Karen over
dinner. But then she shares her news first. A
baby.

"A what?" you say.

"A baby. You know, one of those small humans.
You're not happy?"

"Of course I am," you say. "It's just, I don't
know. I can't see myself that way. I'm a Special
Guest Star. I'm doing better than I ever have, but
I still don't make enough to support a family."

"News flash. I'm doing pretty well myself."

"Oh I know you are."

"I don't know what that means, and we should
talk about that later. But for now, I just want to
ask, why are you ruining this moment, Willis?"

"Oh my God," you say. You are ruining this
moment. You're an idiot. "I'm so sorry." You kiss
Karen's face and neck and face again, you hold

her tight then get worried you're holding her too
tight. You take out your stash of envelopes and
make a decent pile of tens and twenties and you
buy a tiny ring and you get down on one knee and
you ask her to marry you. She says yes.

The two of you get married at the courthouse.
You have a new resolve, throwing yourself into
work. She wonders aloud where you'll all live.
Chinatown? In the SRO?

A month. Two months. A trimester. Another. Then
one more. Then:

You're parents.

You hold your daughter in your arms. She looks
at you and you know that she came from somewhere
else, somewhere beyond your comprehension, the
little tiny interior space you've been living
in, inside your own dumb head. You know she is
an alien from another planet here to save you.
A being from some faraway land. She takes one
look at you and you know that she knows things
about you and you know things about yourself that
you didn't before. You have been a father for
approximately ten seconds and you know for certain
that you will never be the same.

You and Karen name her Phoebe.

Karen and Phoebe and you, in the SRO. You can't
raise this kid here, you think. But for the time
being, until you make it, it'll have to do. All of
you in the room on eight. Cozy. Noisy. The sounds
of the building traveling up the central column.
Hot garbage wafting up in thermal waves. The baby
crying through the night, the neighbors banging

on your floor and ceiling. You do the cop show.
As Ethnic Recurring. The hours are longer but the
envelopes are fatter. You are on the verge. Again.
Like you have been for a while.

You come home one day and Karen's making noises
at the baby. The evening switch-off—she hands the
baby to you, gets ready to go to her job now.

"I have big news," she says, her back turned,
getting dressed for work. She's uncharacteristically
nervous. You can hear it in her voice.

"Okay," you say, "let's hear it." You don't know
why you said it like that. That starts things off
on the wrong note already. Karen knows this is
going to be weird, and on some level, so do you.

"My own show," she says. "A huge role. I'm
playing a young mother." For once it's about her,
as it should be. Breathless, it all comes tumbling
out, the responsibility, how important the role
is, the anchor of the story. She can't contain
herself.

"There's even a part for you in it," she says.
"We can move out of here. Start a new life."

You smile, your face tight. Bounce the baby
gently. Look at her little face.

"Willis," she says. "What do you think?"

"It's great. It's great."

"I know it is. But the fact that you said it like
that makes me think you don't think it is."

"It's great."

"I don't get it. Isn't this what you wanted? To
move out of here?"

"Yeah. I mean, yeah."

"But you wanted to be the one who did it. Is that it? You wanted to be the one who moved us out."

"I'm really close to making it, Karen."

"You've been close for a while."

"You don't believe in me."

"I do believe in you. That's why I don't want to watch you do this anymore."

"You don't think I deserve it."

"Of course you deserve it. You've deserved it for a while. But do you really think they're going to give it to you? Today they say tomorrow. Tomorrow they'll say the next day. I just don't want you to be trapped. Like your father."

"Trapped? What do you know about my father? Do you even know who he was back in the day? You don't get to talk to me about my father. Or being trapped."

"I'm sorry. I'm just saying—"

"It's what's best for our family. I have to stay for now. I've worked too hard to get it. If I get this, I can provide for you, for our kid."

"We don't need you to provide. I can provide. Didn't you hear me say I have my own show? It can be our show together."

"You just don't get it. I don't want to be on your show."

"You resent me. For doing better—"

"Say it. For doing better than I have. But no, that's not it. It's not about you, Karen. It's about me. About becoming Kung Fu Guy."

"Seriously? It's still about that? After all this time?"

"What do you mean? Of course it is. This is the dream. This is what someone like me has available to him. Of course it's still about that."

"There are other things worth pursuing, Willis. The world is out there, and it's big."

"Maybe not for me. I'm sorry, okay? I'm sorry I can't let go of this yet."

"So what are you saying? You don't want to be part of this family?"

"I do. I do, Karen. We can make it work. Like I said, I'm close to getting everything I've worked for, and as soon as I do, things will change. I'll come join your show, but with my own thing. I just need to do this."

"The show's set in the suburbs. Deep. Nowhere near here. Long-distance doesn't work with a kid, Willis."

"Just for a while. A few weeks. Maybe a couple of months."

"A couple of months?"

"Tops."

So she goes. And you keep working. A few weeks turns into a couple of months which turn into several. Several months turns into a year. More. That creeping feeling. Karen was right. Something you've known all along, maybe. It's never going to happen. You should quit now.

A glimmer. A glimpse of a life outside this. And then, perfect timing, right when you start to seriously consider for the first time in your life an existence outside of Chinatown, the phone rings and it's the director and he

says the words you have been waiting to hear all
your life.

Congratulations.

You are:

KUNG FU GUY

No Karen here to share the moment. You're alone.
You got exactly what you wanted. Didn't you? Or
did they give it to you. The thing you thought
you wanted. The role of a lifetime is one you can
never bring yourself to quit. Karen was right: you
are trapped. Doing well *is* the trap. A different
kind, but still a trap. Because you're still in a
show that doesn't have a role for you.

INT. GOLDEN PALACE CHINESE RESTAURANT

You're standing by the food table. It's this
table of food. You can eat the food. No one's
counting. But you also don't want to embarrass
yourself. It's easy to embarrass yourself. They
have everything: little finger sandwiches cut into
triangles or squares, roast beef or smoked turkey
or cucumber tomato for the vegetarians or pretend
vegetarians, heaping mounds of curry chicken salad
and shrimp salad and tarragon pasta salad, all
kinds of foods in stick form, carrot sticks, celery
sticks, zucchini sticks, cubes of cheese (three
colors, although to be honest you can't tell the
difference), and that's not even getting into the
desserts. Pyramids of brownies and blondies and

dainty miniature red velvet cupcakes and vegan
versions of all of the above. Snickerdoodles as
big as your head. Candy, gum, mints, coffee, tea,
soda. Sometimes if the day goes long, they'll bring
out a surprise: Korean tacos stuffed with bulgogi
and kimchi slaw. Handmade ice cream sandwiches.
You're standing there, stuffing greasy cold cuts
into napkins, sneaking balled-up meat bombs into
the pockets of your kung fu pants, a meal that you
can sneak back at the end of the day. You stop to
consider what you are doing. Still playing a part
that was handed to you, written for Asian Man.
You understand: you've made a mistake. The biggest
mistake of your life. Man. You screwed up. You
need to go find your family. How do you get out?
You can't go out the front door. You sneak out the
back.

EXT. ALLEY

You look up at the billboard. BLACK and WHITE.
You can't be a part of this anymore. Their car is
parked there. A getaway car for you—now on the
run. You jimmy the lock, hotwire the ignition,
and you're off. Driving off. Behind you, you hear
sirens. You step on the gas and lose them.

*Local Chinese children
were also dressed as
rural peasants by day to
add to the ambience. By
night they changed back
into their normal Western
clothes.*

Bonnie Tsui

*When . . . an outsider
happens upon a
performance that was
not meant for him . . .
the performers will find
themselves temporarily
torn between two possible
realities.*

Erving Goffman

ACT V
KUNG FU DAD

INT. CHILD'S BEDROOM—MORNING

Upbeat music jangles and jumps!

> SINGING CHILDREN
> We're up, we're up, we're happy.

Phoebe Wu sits up in bed, stretches her arms, her yawning mouth a perfect O.

> SINGING CHILDREN (CONT'D)
> Rise and shine, Phoebe Wu!

INT. BATHROOM—MORNING—MOMENTS LATER

Phoebe, now dressed, brushing her teeth, singing along.

INT. KITCHEN—MORNING—A LITTLE LATER

Phoebe enters the kitchen, singing.

> PHOEBE
> (singing)
> *Xie Xie Mei Mei!*

> SINGING CHILDREN
> (echoing)
> *Xie Xie Mei Mei!*

PHOEBE
Bu iong xie!

Phoebe, backpack on now, lines up with children
of identical heights, large heads and tiny bodies,
bobbing along.

Singing children. Phoebe joins, in step, in key,
as they file into the bus, heads bobbing, off to
school:

SINGING CHILDREN
Xie Xie Mei Mei!
Xie Xie Mei Mei!

It's a cartoon. Sort of.
Real people against an animated backdrop, a
show about a little Chinese girl, Mei Mei (little
sister), and her adventures in a new country.
The country is geographically unique and
logically impossible, some amalgam of dynastic
China, a Taiwanese village in the olden days
(before imperial colonizers!), and some focus-
group-tested, aesthetically engineered, perfect
mythical U.S. suburb. Location, location, location,
three of them, composited into one perfect
synthesis incorporated and flattening, the world
as a children's illustrated atlas, primary colors
and rounded edges, smoothing out the map, blurring
the boundaries and natural barriers, an optimistic
amnesiac's retelling of the age-old story of
immigration, acculturation, assimilation.

Mei Mei can move freely between these places, just by stepping through a doorway, into the next room. Space and time, apparently, being highly malleable, as Mei Mei navigates her new country, learning words for foods, and places, questions ("Where is the bathroom?" and "How much are the squash?"), directions ("Turn left for the police station, turn right for the bank").

Strangers are friendly, for the most part, and why not, given Mei Mei's pink-cheeked post-toddler disposition, precocious for a five-year-old but still innocent enough to not have encountered anyone at school who might make fun of her short-sleeved flowered silk shirt, or, even more likely, recoil at the smell of the fermented black beans in the lunch box her a-kong packed for her.

Xie Xie Mei Mei, you sing.

Xie Xie Mei Mei, the other kids sing.

INT. PHOEBE'S ROOM—MORNING

Phoebe opens the door to see you standing there:

> PHOEBE
>
> Daddy!

> KUNG FU DAD
>
> Phoebe.

> PHOEBE
>
> I haven't seen you in so long.

                    KUNG FU DAD
     I know. I'm sorry.

                      PHOEBE
     I asked Mom why we couldn't visit.
     She said you were busy.

                    KUNG FU DAD
     I missed you.
          (looking around)
     This place is not how I imagined it.

She jumps into you for a quick hug.

                    KUNG FU DAD
     Oof. You got heavy.
          (then)
     Where did the years go?

                    KAREN (O.S.)
     Nice of you to drop by, Will.

Karen appears in the window.

                    KUNG FU DAD
     Karen—wow, holy shit, you look
     great. Like really great.

                      PHOEBE
     Oops Daddy! You said a grown-up
     word!

> SINGING CHILDREN (O.S.)
> He said a grown-up word!

> KUNG FU DAD
> Sorry.
> (to the children)
> I shouldn't have said that.

> KAREN
> Nice of you to say, Will, although
> fairly inappropriate on all
> fronts.

Phoebe is leading the singing children in a
single-file line, getting ready for the next
segment.

> KUNG FU DAD
> (re: Phoebe)
> She's, like, a person now. When
> did she get so big?

> KAREN
> Time flies when you're doing the
> kid show.

> KUNG FU DAD
> It's a lot to process. I just
> learned that my daughter is this
> amazing person.

                    KAREN
We're all learning a lot. But
mostly just you. Speaking of
which:
     (leads children in song)
And now it's learning time!

                  KUNG FU DAD
I don't want to sing.

                    KAREN
Learning time is a special time,
learning time is—

                  KUNG FU DAD
No, seriously.

                    KAREN
Learning is a serious matter. Try
to keep up. You'll figure it out.

                   PHOEBE
So, what are we going to learn
about today?

                  KUNG FU DAD
I . . . don't know. I guess I
could show you some kung fu
moves?

Phoebe laughs. Karen looks concerned.

                    PHOEBE
Haha, Daddy is silly, isn't he?

                    KAREN
     (deadpan)
He sure is. A silly, silly man.

                    PHOEBE
I like kung fu. But we usually
save physical activity for our
Move Your Body segment!

                    KAREN
This is the part where we learn
songs and rhymes with positive
messages about tolerance and
inclusion!

               CHILDREN (O.S.)
Yay!

                    PHOEBE
And culture and food and
vocabulary!

               CHILDREN (O.S.)
Yay! Yay! Yay!

               KUNG FU DAD
Tell me one thing. In this story,
are we together?

                    KAREN
No, Will. That was your choice.

                    PHOEBE
Divorce is a part of life!

                  KUNG FU DAD
        (to Karen)
They talk about divorce on this
show?

                    KAREN
You need to watch more kids'
shows.

                    PHOEBE
I have two parents and they love
me just as much. Now I have two
homes instead of one.

                CHILDREN (O.S.)
Sometimes grown-ups need to make
hard choices!

                    KAREN
Maybe we should talk. Privately.

                  KUNG FU DAD
Is there somewhere we can go?

INT. PHOEBE LAND—GROWN-UP TALKING PLACE

You peek out the window. All clear.

> KAREN
> You just show up here? After all
> this time?

> KUNG FU DAD
> I missed you. I mean her. Phoebe.
> (re: Phoebe Land)
> How did this happen?

> KAREN
> You said you didn't want her to
> grow up in the SRO.

> KUNG FU DAD
> But. This place?

> KAREN
> You lost the right to make that
> decision.
> (then)
> I'm going to leave you to get to
> know your daughter now. If you
> take her outside to play, make
> sure to put sunscreen on her.

A muffled whimper out of Phoebe. She does this
thing, when she gets nervous, a tiny clearing of
her throat, almost a squeak, usually twice, maybe

four times, always in twos. Self-comforting. You
look over at your daughter.

> KUNG FU DAD
> Didn't realize you were there,
> honey.

> PHOEBE
> It's okay.

> KUNG FU DAD
> Also, sorry for being a, uh,
> crappy dad.

> PHOEBE
> It's fine. You tried.

> KUNG FU DAD
> Do you want to play something?

> PHOEBE
> We need to retreat to the castle!

Phoebe runs off, the sobs trailing after her now,
bursting into full-fledged running and crying.

> KUNG FU DAD
> The castle?

INT. CASTLE (AKA PHOEBE'S CLOSET)—DAY

You follow the sound of her talking to herself,
climbing up a tower, the winding staircase
narrowing as it ascends, until you come to a door
just big enough for you to crawl through.
   The door is ajar, and from the room inside, you
catch Phoebe, mid-story.

                    PHOEBE
             (softly, to herself)
          . . . and I'll have a store where
          I sell things I make. I will make
          a comic book and I am going to
          sell it, and if I make something
          else, I will sell it, too. I will
          sell things for a dollar or a
          hundred dollars but if you have
          no money I will sell things to you
          for a penny and you can give me
          the penny whenever or you don't
          have to give me a penny, I will
          sell it to you for no money and I
          will give you a hundred dollars.
          Daddy said he will help me with
          the store . . .

She pauses, for a breath.

                    PHOEBE (CONT'D)
          He is busy working right now but
          he is smart and tall and when he
          is done working on the weekend we

       will work on setting up the store.
       Also at the store we will sell
       stuffed animals and if you buy a
       stuffed animal we will donate the
       proceeds to help animals that get
       killed for their tusks and horns
       like elephants and rhinos . . .

Watching her is like finding old letters, of things you knew thirty years ago and haven't thought of since. How to feel, how to be yourself. Not how to perform or act. How to be.

You survey the room: drawings, hair ties, notes to herself. Seemingly every species of stuffed animal or creature, real or imagined, lined up like a royal court along the walls on the floors. Her friends, her audience. Her off-screen voices. She seems both more resourceful and yet more childlike at the same time—how she's invented a world, stylized, so that its roles and scenery, its characters and rules, its truths and dangers, all fit within one room. How small it is, and overstuffed, and ready for expansion. How bright it is, how messy. This whole place, the objects in it, all from her.

               KUNG FU DAD
       You made all of this.

                PHOEBE
    (shy)
    Yeah.

                    KUNG FU DAD
How did you do it?

                    PHOEBE
Do what?

                    KUNG FU DAD
Build a castle. Build a whole
world.

                    PHOEBE
Oh. Like this.

She shows you, using what she has. Small rounded
kid scissors. Scraps of fabric. Glue, tape, a binder
clip, some string. Strips of paper on which she
labels her world, names for everything written
carefully in neat cursive that wanders around the
page.
   She pauses. She's a thoughtful kid. Already
better at this than you are. You can already see
the day when you'll have aged into your next role,
when you'll put on the old-man suit. You'll fumble,
feeling the future slip away, and she'll still be
young, moving away from you with every moment.

                    PHOEBE
     The thing about building a castle
     in the air is it's easy. You build
     up. It's like a little ladder, then
     you start building a castle in the
     air. Then, you destroy the ladder.
     And your castle is floating.

                    KUNG FU DAD
Why do you need the ladder in the
first place?

                       PHOEBE
Dad!

                    KUNG FU DAD
Sorry. Is that a dumb question?

                       PHOEBE
There are no dumb questions.

                   CHILDREN (O.S.)
There are no dumb questions!

                    KUNG FU DAD
Thanks honey. And thanks, weird
children that I am unable to see.

                       PHOEBE
You can't just build in the air.

                    KUNG FU DAD
Right. Of course.

                       PHOEBE
It's not connected to anything.
So you build a bridge to the air,
then you can break that bridge.
But nothing falls down.

                    KUNG FU DAD
       Makes sense. That's cool.

                      PHOEBE
       See, this is a big pig face I
       built in the air. It's a huge head
       of a huge pig and it's huge.

                    KUNG FU DAD
       I like that.

Phoebe smiles. Then frowns.

                      PHOEBE
       Okay, I'm done with this. I want
       to draw now.

                    KUNG FU DAD
       I'll watch you draw.

                      PHOEBE
       I don't feel like drawing anymore.
       I just want to sit with you here.

                    KUNG FU DAD
       That's okay, too.

The words coming out of your mouth, you can feel
it happening, how you're softening, changing into
a different person. You were a bit player in the
world of Black and White, but here and now, in
her world, you're more. Not the star of the show,

something better. The star's dad. Somehow you were
lucky enough to end up in her story.

INT. PHOEBE'S ROOM—NIGHT

The truth is, she's a weirdo. Just like you were.
Are. A glorious, perfectly weird weirdo. Like all
kids before they forget how to be exactly how
weird they really are. Into whatever they're into,
pure. Before knowing. Before they learn from others
how to act. Before they learn they are Asian, or
Black, or Brown, or White. Before they learn about
all the things they are and about all the things
they will never be.

> PHOEBE
> Wanna know what I'm afraid of?

> KUNG FU DAD
> Sure.

> PHOEBE
> I'm afraid of five things.

> KUNG FU DAD
> Only five?

> PHOEBE
> Five is a lot!

> KUNG FU DAD
> Okay, let's hear them.

                    PHOEBE
     Secret passages.

                    KUNG FU DAD
     That's one.

                    PHOEBE
     Waking up sweaty.
     Getting eaten by a witch.

                    KUNG FU DAD
     Two and three.

                    PHOEBE
     A pebble flying into your eye.

                    KUNG FU DAD
     That's a good one.

She pauses.

                    KUNG FU DAD
     We're only up to four so far.

                    PHOEBE
     I know.

                    KUNG FU DAD
     What's five?

                    PHOEBE
     I don't want to say.

                    KUNG FU DAD
Why not? Just say it. I won't be
mad.

                    PHOEBE
Okay.
    (then)
My dad dying.

                    KUNG FU DAD
You don't have to worry.
I'm very tough.

She looks at him, confused.

                    PHOEBE
Everyone dies, Daddy. You live
until you're one hundred. You turn
one hundred and then you die.

                    KUNG FU DAD
Let's go with that.

She seems satisfied. For the moment.

                    PHOEBE
Can you tell me a story?

                    KUNG FU DAD
I don't know how. No one's ever
asked me to.

                    PHOEBE
        Can you try?

                  KUNG FU DAD
        Okay. I'll try.
            (deep breath)
        There once was a little girl who
        was—

You pause. Unsure of what to say next.

This is a key point in the story.

The next word, and whatever you say after that,
will determine a great many things about it, will
either open up the story, like a key in a lock
in a door to a palace with however many rooms,
too many to count, and hallways and stairways and
false walls and secret passages, or the next word
could be a wall itself, two walls, closing in, it
could be limits on where the story could go.

You search for the right word, the pressure and
expectation from her little face mounting with each
millisecond of silence that passes, and it is about
to come to your lips and tongue, you are just
about to say it when your daughter turns to you
and says—

                    PHOEBE
        It's okay, Daddy.

                    KUNG FU DAD
It is?

                    PHOEBE
Yeah. I can tell you don't want to
right now.

                    KUNG FU DAD
No no, I have one. Here it goes.

                    PHOEBE
Wait!

She tucks herself tightly under her blanket, up to
her neck, so she's just a head, two big blinking
eyes. You study her features, see bits of yourself
in there, but thank God, much more Karen.

                    KUNG FU DAD
Ready?

                    PHOEBE
Ready!

                    KUNG FU DAD
This is a story about a guy.

                    PHOEBE
I like where this is going.

                    KUNG FU DAD
This guy, something weird happened
to him.

                        PHOEBE
Weird things happen to me all the
time. Yesterday, two of my toes
got stuck together for a whole
minute.

                    KUNG FU DAD
That is weird.

                        PHOEBE
So weird.

                    KUNG FU DAD
Are they okay now?

                        PHOEBE
I unstuck them.

                    KUNG FU DAD
That's a relief.

                        PHOEBE
Dad?

                    KUNG FU DAD
Yes?

                        PHOEBE
I'm getting sleepy.

And then the children start singing softly, an
indistinct chorus of sounds, together sounding
like a lullaby. She falls asleep, and you watch her

for a minute, stroke her cheek. When the
sun is all the way down, you rouse her for the
nightly routine, following the music cues,
learning to be a parent on the fly, out of
necessity, winging it, getting help from
imaginary beings and strange neighbors who are
weirdly judgmental but ultimately helpful. Your
kung fu is useless here.

Instead, this. A kind of dream. Her own bedroom,
her own bed. Her own yard. Without a restaurant
downstairs, or sirens or cops or dead bodies.
No fishy garbage fumes, or flumes of mildewing
vegetation, no cacophony of five dialects being
smashed together, a solid block of sensory
overload rising up the dank central corridor of
INT. CHINATOWN SRO. Instead, PHOEBE LAND. This
place, without Generic Asian Men, unshaven,
sweating through their yellowing undershirts, no
Hostess/Prostitutes, no Old Asian People with
their weird breath and liver spots and
interminable wandering remembrances of the
old village and hardship and how they got there.
None of that. Just songs and flowers and
upbeat jangles and jumps. She lives here,
without history, unaware of all that came before,
and who are you to say that this isn't the end
point, this wasn't the goal all along, that
Chinese Railroad Worker and Opium Den Dragon
Lady and Kimono Girl and Striving Immigrant and
Honorable Dead Asian Guy and Kung Fu Guy weren't
all leading to *Xie Xie Mei Mei*? To this dream of
assimilation, a dream finally realized, a real
American girl.

INT. PHOEBE'S ROOM—NIGHT

You do mealtime, you do bedtime. No kung fu. Just
spaghetti, and broccoli. PJs and story. Brush.
Floss. Pee. Glass of water. Feed your fishes. Okay.
Okay. Kiss kiss. Wait! What? You didn't kiss the
baby lion. Where is the baby lion? I don't know.
Oh come on. Here it is. Okay, I kissed it. And the
hamster dog. And the hamster dog. All of them are
kissed. Okay. Night night. Stop talking. I'm not
talking. Stop whispering. Phoebe, really, no more.
She washes her face. Small, chubby hands, holding
the soap. Scrubbing her cheeks and forehead with
her soft baby hands. It looks familiar and then
you understand. That's how you do it. She's been
watching you. Learning. Brush. Floss. Pee. Glass
of water. Feed your fishes. Kiss the baby lion.
Kiss the hamster dog. Kiss, kiss. Finally, after
what feels like months without a break, the moon
comes out, with its creepy but sweet moon face, the
sun closes its eyes and sinks down to the painted
horizon, and Phoebe, along with the rest of Phoebe
Land, goes to sleep.

INT. PHOEBE LAND—NIGHT

You lie awake, staring through a small open
window at a full blue moon, complete with a silly
face. This is the dream. Sustainable employment.
Some semblance of work-life balance. Talk white.
Not a lot. Get contact lenses. Smile. They will
assume you're smart. The less you say, the

better. Try to project: Responsible, Harmless. An
unthreatening amount of color sprinkled in. That's
the dream, a dream of blending in. A dream of
going from Generic Asian Man to just plain
Generic Man. To settle down. To stay here. But
you can't stay here forever. This isn't real.
It's just another role. You can't, you can't, you
can't. Can you?

You go to the window, peek out.

                    KAREN
          Is everything okay?

                    PHOEBE
          The police?

                    KUNG FU DAD
          Don't be scared. They're here
          for me.

                    PHOEBE
          I'm scared.

                    KUNG FU DAD
          I'm ready. I've been waiting for
          this.

The sirens stop. From a megaphone, a voice you
recognize.

                    TURNER
          Come out with your hands up.

                    PHOEBE
Daddy no. No. No.

                    GREEN
Give yourself up and no one gets
hurt.

                    PHOEBE
Are you going to jail, Daddy?
   (to Karen)
Is Daddy going to jail?

                    KAREN
No, sweetie. Daddy is going to
prison.

                  KUNG FU DAD
It'll be okay honey. This is a
good thing.

                    PHOEBE
Prison is a good thing?

                  CHILDREN (O.S.)
Prison is not usually a good
thing!

                  KUNG FU DAD
In this case it is.

                    KAREN
I don't understand. How did they
find you here?

                    KUNG FU DAD
        I might have stolen Turner's car.

                      KAREN
        They tracked the vehicle.

She laughs. You laugh.

                      KAREN
        You wanted them to find you.

                    KUNG FU DAD
        I wanted them to find us.

ACT VI
THE CASE OF THE MISSING ASIAN

EXHIBIT A

LAWS OF THE UNITED STATES

1859 *Oregon's constitution is revised: no
"Chinaman" can own property in the state.*

1879 *California's constitution is revised:
ownership of land is limited to aliens of
"the white race or of African descent."*

1882 *On May 6, the U.S. (Federal) Chinese Exclusion
Act is signed into law by President Chester A.
Arthur, prohibiting all immigration of Chinese
laborers, the first law preventing all members
of a specific ethnic or national group from
immigrating into the United States.*

1886 *Washington Territory's constitution bars
aliens ineligible for citizenship from owning
property.*

1890 *In the City of San Francisco, the Bingham
Ordinance prohibits Chinese people (whether
or not U.S. citizens) from either working
or living in San Francisco, except in "a
portion set apart for the location of all the
Chinese," thereby creating a literal, legally
defined ghetto.*

1892   *The U.S. (Federal) Geary Act requires all Chinese residents of the United States to carry a permit, failure to carry such permit (at any time) being punishable by deportation or one year of hard labor. In addition, Chinese are not allowed to bear witness in court.*

1920   *The U.S. (Federal) Cable Act decrees that any American woman who marries "an alien ineligible for citizenship shall cease to be a citizen of the United States."*

1924   *U.S. (Federal) Immigration Act of 1924, also known as the Johnson-Reed Act, limits the number of immigrants allowed entry into the United States through a national origins quota. **It completely prohibits immigration from Asia.***

INT. COURTROOM

You're seated at the defendant's table, wearing
the only suit you own. The one you got married in.
Still fits, mostly.

Your lawyer walks in. It's Older Brother.

>   YOU
>   Huh?

>   OLDER BROTHER
>   Hey Will. You been working out?

You stand up, shake his hand. Older Brother pulls
you in for a hug.

>   YOU
>   Where have you been?

>   OLDER BROTHER
>   You serious?

>   YOU
>   Yeah.

>   OLDER BROTHER
>   Law school.

>   YOU
>   Oh. Right.

OLDER BROTHER
How is he?

YOU
Sifu?

OLDER BROTHER
He need money?

YOU
Nah. I mean, yeah. But nah.

OLDER BROTHER
All of those roles. He never got a
story.

YOU
You were the story. Supposed
to be.

OLDER BROTHER
I know that's what everyone
wanted. A kung fu hero. But I
couldn't.

YOU
I think I'm starting to understand
what you mean.

OLDER BROTHER
I never left. Not really. Not in
the way that counts—inside. In my
mind. Another part of me is in

a different place now. Interior
Chinatown isn't the whole world
anymore. I had to leave in my own
way. Just like you tried to do.

A door opens. Commotion in the gallery. Lawyers
shuffle papers. The judge enters the courtroom.
Stares you down.
  Green and Turner in the first row, just behind
you, ready to testify for the prosecution. The
judge smiles at them.

                    BAILIFF
All rise. Case No. 47311, *People*
vs. Wu.
    (then)
The Case of the Missing Asian.

                     YOU
Hey.

                OLDER BROTHER
Yeah.

                     YOU
Did you do well in law school?

                OLDER BROTHER
Really? Come on, Willis.
    (flashes a winning smile)
I was editor-in-chief of the
law review. Or did you forget
who I am?

                    JUDGE
        The prosecution will call its
        first witness.

The assistant DA, brilliant and hard-charging and
also has this incredible head of hair, auburn or
chestnut, sexy in her crisp navy pantsuit, looks
like she stepped out of an ad for navy pantsuits,
rises, heads toward the witness stand. Older
Brother also rises.

                OLDER BROTHER
        Objection.

                    JUDGE
        Objection to what?

                OLDER BROTHER
        Your Honor, we object to all of
        this. The whole thing. This mock
        trial. The entire justice system
        is rigged against my client.

                    JUDGE
        Let me get this straight. Your
        objection, presented to the court
        and to me as its arbiter, is to the
        very legitimacy of the body you
        are presenting that objection to.

                OLDER BROTHER
        When you put it that way it does
        sound a little silly.

                    PROSECUTION
The prosecution rests, Your Honor.

                      JUDGE
You can't rest. You haven't
presented your case yet.

                    PROSECUTION
Based on what's going on right
now, we're feeling pretty good
about our chances.

                      JUDGE
Noted. Nevertheless, as a matter
of law, you have the burden of
proof. You need to present some
kind of case.

                    PROSECUTION
Ugh. Fine. The prosecution calls
Miles Turner to the stand.

Turner is wearing a charcoal gray suit, very faint
pinstripes, cut for his build. He takes the stand,
clenches a couple of times. The bailiff almost
faints.

                PROSECUTION (CONT'D)
State your name and rank.

                      TURNER
Detective Miles Turner.

His pec flexes under his shirt. Involuntary?
Maybe.

> PROSECUTION
> Detective, you've been
> investigating the Case of the
> Missing Asian, correct?

> TURNER
> That's correct.

> PROSECUTION
> And in that time, you have had
> opportunity to observe Mr. Wu.

> TURNER
> I've had opportunity to observe
> that he's a punk.

> OLDER BROTHER
> Your Honor, come on.

> JUDGE
> (to Turner)
> Detective, I'll caution you to
> keep your comments professional
> and, more important, relevant to
> the matter at hand.

> TURNER
> Fine. He's not a punk. He's a
> weenie.

                    OLDER BROTHER
Objection.

                     PROSECUTION
Is that your only move? Let me
guess, you got an A in Objections
at law school.

                    OLDER BROTHER
             (to judge)
I don't see how my client being a
weenie is relevant.

                        YOU
Can we stop referring to me as a
weenie?

                     PROSECUTION
Your Honor, I will establish
relevance. If only defense counsel
would stop objecting.

                       JUDGE
Okay, I'll allow it. For now. But
you better get to the point, fast.
             (then)
That's a beautiful pantsuit.

                     PROSECUTION
             (giggles)
Thank you, Your Honor.

                    OLDER BROTHER
                 (under his breath)
          Uh oh.

                        YOU
          Why did you say uh oh?

                    PROSECUTION
          Now then, Detective, how is it
          relevant, your observation of
          Mr. Wu's character?

                      TURNER
          He's internalized a sense of
          inferiority. To White people,
          obviously. But also to Black
          people. Does he realize that?

          A pause. Silence. All eyes in the courtroom turn
          to you.

                      TURNER
          He thinks he can't participate in
          this race dialogue, because Asians
          haven't been persecuted as much as
          Black people.
                      (to you)
          Don't you need to take some
          responsibility for yourself? For
          the categories you put us in?
          Black and White? I mean, come on?
          Do you think you're the only one
          who's trapped?

Your cheeks flush, your foot starts twitching.

> PROSECUTION
> Thank you, Detective. No further
> questions. Prosecution calls to
> the stand Detective Sarah Green.

Green takes the stand. The prosecutor makes eyes
at her.

> GREEN
> Detective Sarah Green, with the
> Impossible Crimes Unit.

> PROSECUTION
> Oh, I know who you are, Detective
> Green.

> OLDER BROTHER
> Objection, Your Honor.

> JUDGE
> What now?

> OLDER BROTHER
> There's too much tension in the
> courtroom. It's way too sexy in
> here.

> JUDGE
> That's a problem because?

OLDER BROTHER
For starters, it could influence
Detective Green's testimony.

The judge leans back, considers this.

JUDGE
Eh. I'll allow it.

OLDER BROTHER
(to you)
We might be screwed.

YOU
I thought you were a good lawyer.
You should have stuck to kung fu.

PROSECUTION
Detective, I just have one
question for you.

GREEN
Go for it.

PROSECUTION
What are you doing for dinner
tonight?

OLDER BROTHER
Okay, that's, that's, I don't even
know what's going on. I move for
an immediate mistrial.

                    JUDGE
Quit with the grandstanding. That
stuff only works on TV.

                    GREEN
Can I say something?

                    JUDGE
Of course you can. Anything you
want. Would you like to sit up
here with me? In the judge's
chair?

                OLDER BROTHER
That's definitely not allowed. This
is literally a sham.

                    GREEN
     (to you)
What are you looking for? Do you
think you're the only group to be
invisible?
How about:
Older women
Older people in general
People that are overweight
People that don't conform to
conventional Western beauty
standards
Black women
Women in general in the workplace
Are you sure you're not looking

for something that you feel
entitled to? Isn't this a kind of
narcissism?
  (then)
Are you sure you're not asking to
be treated like a White man?

                OLDER BROTHER
He's asking to be treated like
an American. A real American.
Because, honestly, when you think
American, what color do you see?
White? Black?
  (dramatic pause)
We've been here two hundred years.
The first Chinese came in 1815.
Germans and Dutch and Irish and
Italians who came at the turn of
the twentieth century. They're
Americans.
  (points at himself)
Why doesn't this face register as
American?
Is it because we make the story
too complicated? Because we
haven't figured out how yet.
Whether it's a tragedy or a comedy
or something in between. If we
haven't cracked the code of what
it's like to be inside this face,
then how can we explain it to
anyone else?

PROSECUTION
Objection. Who cares?

JUDGE
Sustained.

OLDER BROTHER
Can I ask a question then?

JUDGE
Go ahead.

OLDER BROTHER
This is the Case of the Missing
Asian, right?

JUDGE
Yes. What's your point?

OLDER BROTHER
If I was the Asian who disappeared,
and now I'm back and standing here
and obviously okay, and there is
a clear and plausible explanation
for where I was—at Harvard Law
School—then what is my client on
trial for?

PROSECUTION
   (rises)
There was another guy who
disappeared.

                    OLDER BROTHER
Who?

                        JUDGE
        (points at you)
You.

                         YOU
I'm on trial for my own
disappearance?

                    OLDER BROTHER
Welcome to Black and White.

                         YOU
Am I the suspect? Or the victim?

                        JUDGE
That's what we're here to decide.
Prosecution may call its next
witness.

                    PROSECUTION
Prosecution rests, Your Honor.

Commotion in the courtroom. Ominous music.

                        JUDGE
    Great. Moving right along. Defense
    will call its first witness.

Older Brother looks at you.

                    OLDER BROTHER
You ready for this?

                         YOU
I am. Also, do I really have a
choice?

                    OLDER BROTHER
You do know kung fu. And I can
still fight. We could just kick
our way out of here.

                         YOU
Let's call that Plan B.

                    OLDER BROTHER
Defense calls to the stand
Mr. Willis Wu, aka Generic Asian
Man Number Three/Delivery Guy, aka
Generic Asian Man Number Two, aka
Kung Fu Guy, aka Kung Fu Dad.

As you walk across the room, you look out into
the gallery, which has tripled in size and is now
overflowing out into the hallway. It seems like
all of the SRO is in here now.

                    OLDER BROTHER
State your name.

                         YOU
Willis Wu.

OLDER BROTHER
Mr. Wu, is it true that you
have an internalized sense of
inferiority?

YOU
What?

OLDER BROTHER
That because on the one hand you,
for obvious reasons, have not been
and can never be fully assimilated
into mainstream, i.e., White
America—

YOU
Dude, what are you saying?

OLDER BROTHER
And on the other hand neither
do you feel fully justified in
claiming solidarity with other
historically and currently
oppressed groups. That while
your community's experience in
the United States has included
racism on the personal and the
institutional levels, including
but not limited to: immigration
quotas, actual federal legislation
expressly excluding people who
look like you from entering
the country. Legislation that

was in effect for almost a
century. Antimiscegenation laws.
Discriminatory housing policies.
Alien land laws and restrictive
covenants. Violation of civil
liberties including internment.
That despite all of that, you
somehow feel that your oppression,
because it does not include the
original American sin—of slavery—
that it will never add up to
something equivalent. That the
wrongs committed against your
ancestors are incommensurate in
magnitude with those committed
against Black people in America.
And whether or not that
quantification, whether accurate
or not, because of all of this
you feel on some level that you
maybe can't even quite verbalize,
out of shame or embarrassment,
that the validity and volume
of your complaints must be
calibrated appropriately, must be
in proportion to the aggregate
suffering of your people.
    (then)
Your oppression is second-class.

                    YOU
Which side are you on?

                    JUDGE
It's a fair question, counselor.

                 OLDER BROTHER
Your Honor, I'm building a defense
for my client, based on his
particular predicament.

                    JUDGE
What predicament is that?

                 OLDER BROTHER
Someone who can't be viewed
through either lens. Whose case
cannot be properly considered
by this court, where the rules
and assumptions are based on a
particular dialectic. Someone
whose story will never fit into
Black and White.
    (then)
The error in your reasoning is
built right into the premise—
using the Black experience as the
model for the Asian immigrant
is necessarily going to lead to
this. It's based on an analogy,
on a comparison, on something
quantitative.

But the experience of Asians in
America isn't just a scaled-back

or dialed-down version of the
Black experience. Instead of co-
opting someone else's experience
or consciousness, he must define
his own.
(then)
I would draw the court's attention
to the case of *People v. Hall*.

SUPREME COURT OF THE STATE OF CALIFORNIA (1854)

People v. Hall

Hugh C. Murray of the Cal S. Ct. ruled that the
Act of April 16, 1850, Section 14, which forbade
"Blacks and Indians" from testifying in favor of or
against a white man, was applicable to the Chinese,
who were legally Indians because both groups were
descended from the same Asiatic ancestors.

From the opinion of California Supreme Court
Justice H. C. Murray:

When Columbus first landed upon the shores
of this continent . . .

he imagined that he had accomplished the
object of his expedition, and that the
Island of San Salvador was one of those
islands of the Chinese Sea lying near the
extremity of India . . .

Acting upon the hypothesis, he gave to the Islanders the name Indian. From that time . . .

The American Indian and the Mongolian or Asiatic, were regarded as the same type of human species.

> OLDER BROTHER
> Murray's reasoning here is breathtaking in its twisted audacity. The legitimacy of categorizing "Asiatics" in such a way as to justify lumping them into the clause "Blacks and Indians" (in order to deny them the right to testify against Whites) is based on the subjective state of mind of a single man (Christopher Columbus) at a particular historical moment hundreds of years ago, who happened at that moment to be spectacularly and egregiously mistaken about where on the globe he had drifted into; thus a navigational misunderstanding of the world itself becomes the justification for a legally binding category.

> JUDGE
> Basically, a mistake.

OLDER BROTHER

Exactly. To put it another way,
because in 1492 Columbus had no
clue where he was, Chinese should
have the same rights as Blacks,
which is to say, no rights. Forget
that this is likely a fiction—even
taking the argument seriously on
its face, the effect of this is
that we have codified with the
force of law a category: Blacks
and Asiatics, separating them
(because obviously, creating a
new category of non-White), a
secondary effect is that it also
codifies Asiatics as outside the
Black category.
Inferior, and yet not in the
same way Blacks were considered
inferior.

The judge leans forward, listening now. Green and
Turner, and even the prosecutor, too. Older Brother
has their attention. Someone in the gallery yells,
you tell 'em, OB.

JUDGE

Order. I'll have order in my
court.

OLDER BROTHER

Somehow, in two hundred years,
every wave, every new boatload of

Asians, still as fresh, as alien
to this land as the first.
  (then)
This is it. The root of it all.
The real history of yellow people
in America. Two hundred years of
being perpetual foreigners.

Older Brother pauses. Takes a sip of water. Not in
a rush at all. Cool as ever. Your heart, on the
other hand, is pounding so hard you think it might
be visible through your shirt. What is everyone
thinking? How can he be saying all of this, in
open court, in front of Black and White and the
American justice system? And yet—no one's kicked
him out. Yet.

                OLDER BROTHER (CONT'D)
They zoned us, kept us roped
off from everyone else. Trapped
us inside. Cut us off from our
families, our history. So we made
it our own place. Chinatown.
A place for preservation and
self-preservation.
Give them what they feel is
right, is safe. Make it fit their
ideas of what is out there. Don't
threaten them. Chinatown and
indeed being Chinese is and always
has been, from the very beginning,
a construction, a performance
of features, gestures, culture,

and exoticism. An invention,
a reinvention, a stylization.
Figuring out the show, finding
our place in it, which was the
background, as scenery, as
nonspeaking players. Figuring
out what you're allowed to say.
Above all, trying to never, ever
offend. To watch the mainstream,
find out what kind of fiction they
are telling themselves, find a
bit part in it. Be appealing and
acceptable, be what they want
to see.
    (then)
My client was a part of this
system. Both victim and suspect,
he killed countless Asian men.
    (gasp from the gallery)
Killed them and then, six weeks
later, became them again, as if
nothing had happened, as if he
had no memory or remorse. He
allowed it to happen, allowed
himself to become Generic, so
that no one could even tell what
was happening. He is guilty, Your
Honor, and ladies and gentlemen
of the jury. Guilty of wanting to
be part of something that never
wanted him.
    (beat)
The defense rests.

Silence. Then: applause. Hooting and hollering
from everyone. It's like the casino and karaoke
night and a party in the SRO all at once—raucous
laughter and unfiltered emotion. Someone said
it. Someone stood up and said all the shit that
we never say, didn't even know how to say. Older
Brother to the rescue, after all, fulfilling his
destiny with his mouth and his brain instead of
his hands and feet.

You look back to see if Sifu is in the
courtroom. You see Old Asian Woman. But you don't
see him. Where is he?

                    JUDGE
        The court will now recess while
        the jury deliberates.

The jury files out.

Green and Turner approach your table.

                    TURNER
            (to Older Brother)
        You should come work for the DA.

                OLDER BROTHER
        Thanks. But I'm good.

                    GREEN
            (to you)
        Good luck, Willis.

When it's finally empty in the courtroom, you turn
to Older Brother.

> YOU
>
> Wow.

> OLDER BROTHER
>
> Are you happy with your
> representation?

> YOU
>
> I mean, yeah. The way you talked
> about history and all that.

> OLDER BROTHER
>
> You have no idea what I was
> saying, do you?

> YOU
>
> Absolutely none. Seriously no
> clue.

Older Brother laughs. Nice to see him crack a
smile.

> YOU (CONT'D)
>
> Just the fact that you stood up
> there, inside this building, in an
> American courtroom, and argued my
> case.

> OLDER BROTHER
>
> Our case. I hope it was enough.

He goes out to the vending machine, buys you each
a soda.

                    OLDER BROTHER
            To our day in court.

You gulp down the can, just now realizing how
tense you are. Ears still buzzing, heart still
racing.

The jury's already coming back. Everyone hurries
back into the courtroom to hear the verdict. The
jurors file back in. The foreperson steps up.

                        YOU
                (whispering)
            That seemed quick.

                    OLDER BROTHER
            Yeah.

                        YOU
            What does that mean?

                    OLDER BROTHER
            I don't know.

                        YOU
            What does it usually mean?

                    OLDER BROTHER
            I don't think that's relevant. I've
            never defended someone for self-

imprisonment before. Guess we'll
find out.

>   JUDGE
> The forewoman will read the verdict.

>   FOREWOMAN
> Your Honor, in the case of *People
> vs. Wu* aka Generic Asian Man, we
> the jury of the people find the
> defendant:
> Guilty as charged.

>   OLDER BROTHER
> This is bullshit.

The courtroom erupts into chaos. The judge bangs
his gavel to no avail. The bailiff has his hand on
his weapon.

>   JUDGE
> Order! Order! People! Settle
> down or I will find you all in
> contempt.
>   (then, to you)
> Before I sentence you, do you have
> anything to say for yourself,
> Mr. Wu?

You look at Older Brother. He nods.

You rise, face the prosecutor, Turner and
Green, the judge, and, most important, all of

the assembled onlookers in the gallery. Up
front, all of you, on trial together. The Generic
Asian Men.

                    YOU
         Ever since I was a boy, I've
         dreamt of being Kung Fu Guy.
            (then)
         Man, my throat is dry again. I
         need water. Can I have water?

Turner comes over, hands you a bottle.

                    YOU
         Thanks.
            (you down the whole bottle)
         Ever since I was a boy, I've
         dreamt of being Kung Fu Guy.
         I practiced all those years,
         dreaming of tomorrow, of the next
         day, of the day it would come.
         And then one day, finally, after
         waiting however many decades for
         it, after how many nights staring
         at the ceiling or my poster of
         Bruce Lee or hearing Sifu's words
         in my head, I finally got my shot.
         And when I did, you know what?
         I thought: I wonder why I wanted
         this so bad.

Murmurs from the gallery. The Generic Asian Men
look confused. So do the Cheuks, and the Monk, and

the Hostess, and the Emperor and all of the Asian
Gangsters.

                    TURNER
          They used you guys. Against us.
          Against yourselves.

Older Brother seems to understand, nodding along.
Old Asian Woman, too—a twinkle in her eye. You
finally got it. She sees it. You finally understood
what she meant.

                    YOU
          Kung Fu Guy is just another form
          of Generic Asian Man.

You've never really given a monologue before. The
lights go down, except for the one on you. The
light, it's on you, and it's hitting you just right.

                    YOU (CONT'D)
            (deep breath)
          We're all the same. Aren't we?
          Generic Asian Man. Maybe I'm Kung
          Fu Guy at the moment, but I know
          as well as you all do that this
          is about half a rung above jack
          shit and I'm about one flubbed
          line from being busted back down
          to the background pool. It sucks
          being Generic Asian Man.

A couple of affirmative grunts.

                    YOU (CONT'D)
But at the same time, I'm
guilty, too. Guilty of playing
this role. Letting it define
me. Internalizing the role so
completely that I've lost track
of where reality starts and the
performance begins. And letting
that define how I see other
people. I'm as guilty of it as
anyone. Fetishizing Black people
and their coolness. Romanticizing
White women. Wishing I were a
White man. Putting myself into
this category.

You find Karen's eyes in the gallery.

                    YOU (CONT'D)
By putting ourselves below
everyone, we're building in a
self-defense mechanism. Protecting
against real engagement. By
imagining that no one wants us,
that all others are so different
from us, we're privileging our own
point of view.
        (surveys crowd)
Look at all of you here. We got
our surfers there . . . our
b-boys. Floppy-haired emo guys.
Clean fade lowered-car guys. Tats,
no tats. All of the varieties of

the Asian American male. Most
of us between five-six and five-
eleven. On some level . . . we do
share something. Played NES and
D&D in middle school. Our moms
make the same foods, frying up
radish and taro cakes, a dollop
of hot stuff and a splash of soy
sauce. Snack time. Our houses
smell the same way, have the same
embarrassing piles of clutter,
with random-ass Asian shit mixed
in with plastic toys and free crap
and a mishmash of furniture and
decor . . .

A couple of mm-hmms, guys climbing on board now.

> YOU (CONT'D)
> . . . and bad carpet and so many
> styles because it all equals
> no style, because decor is not
> something our parents care
> about or can afford. Matching
> pillows and shit, that's for White
> people. Our shit is functional,
> like a table is where you eat
> and do homework. And get good
> grades and be well rounded in
> extracurriculars and get into an
> Ivy or a good state school and
> then you graduate with a solid
> GPA and you come out here and

find out that what you are
is . . . Asian Man. But how
often do you, or you, or any of
us ever think the thought, I'm
an Asian man? Almost never. Not
until someone reminds you. Some
guy bumps you at a bar, and makes
a comment. Or you overhear some
people talking, and one of them
says, oh, your Asian friend so-
and-so. And in that moment, we
all become the same again. All
of us collapse into one, Generic
Asian Man.
   (then)
What I'm trying to say is, we
aren't Generic Asian Men. I mean,
look at us. We look ridiculous.
All pretending to be the same
thing. We're not.
   (pointing out guys in the
   crowd)
Choy, you know what I'm talking
about. Fong. And you, you
definitely know what I mean, right
Carl?

          NOT CARL
I'm not Carl.

          YOU
Sorry. You get my point.

                    NOT CARL
     I do. But I wish you knew my name.
     We went to junior high together.

                      YOU
     I'm sorry, man. My point is, I'm
     looking out at all of you. And my
     parents, our elders, my friends.
        (then)
     At my daughter.

Old Asian Woman looks at you, then at Phoebe and
Karen.

                      YOU
     I'm looking at my wife. Ex-wife.
     But maybe ex-ex-wife?

Karen looks at you. She smiles. And frowns. And
smiles a little bit.

                    KAREN
     You're sort of losing the thread
     here, Will.

                      YOU
     Right. Thanks.

                    KAREN
     I love you, though.

YOU (CONT'D)
And I just want to say one thing
to all of you. The truth is, I am
guilty. It's my fault. The question
isn't where did the Asian guy
disappear to?

The question is: why is the Asian
guy always dead?

Because we don't fit. In the
story. If someone showed you my
picture on the street, how would
you describe it?

You might say, an Asian fellow.
Asian dude. Asian Man.

How many of you would say: that's
an American?

What is it about an Asian Man
that makes him so hard to
assimilate?

Grunts from the gallery.

YOU (CONT'D)
Why doesn't he have a role in
Black and White?

The question is:

Who gets to be an American? What
does an American look like?

We're trapped as guest stars in
a small ghetto on a very special
episode. Minor characters locked
into a story that doesn't quite
know what to do with us. After two
centuries here, why are we still
not Americans? Why do we keep
falling out of the story?

More grunts. Some mm-hmns. A "hell yeah."

                    YOU (CONT'D)
          I spent most of my life trapped.
          Interior Chinatown. I made it out,
          to become Kung Fu Dad. But that
          was just another role. A better
          role than I've ever had, but still
          a role. I can't just keep doing
          the same thing over and over
          again. My dad did that. And
          where did it get him? He was a
          true master, someone who had
          mastered his craft. And what did
          his life add up to? You never
          recognized him for what he could
          do. Who he was. You never allowed
          him a name.

          So what do we do?

You look at Older Brother.

The gallery is fired up now. Angry Asians. The
judge bangs his gavel, order order, but no one's
listening. It's about to explode.

> OLDER BROTHER
>
> Plan B?

> YOU
>
> Plan B.

The music kicks in. A dozen cops come busting
through the door, three from the front, one from
the back, and one from upstairs. You take your
stance. Older Brother next to you. Come on, you
say. Come get this. You fight off the first wave,
a bunch of slow-moving grunts, but then another
wave. Then another. The SWAT team arrives. All
the Generic Asian Men jump in now. It's a melee.
In all of the action, you find it: the thing Sifu
told you. One thing. One thing a day. One thing
at a time. Everything slows down, the music fades
away, and it's just breathing. Your breathing, and
the sound of skin on skin, skin on bone, crunch
and slap. Your kung fu is free, is flowing, is at
a level it could never have reached, in all those
years. Up block, side step, body punch, side kick,
down block, down block. Jump, clear the counter,
push off, SPLITS IN THE AIR, kicking two dudes
at once, one in the face, one in the throat, who
did that? You can jump like this, landing, no-look
back kick, guy goes down with a liquid-y sound,

like he's a bag of organs, the energy from your
foot in a strike point, radiating outward and who
the hell are you, and this is not B or B-plus or
even A-minus kung fu. Six feet above the ground,
somersaults in the air, butterfly kicks, twisting
horizontally, diagonally, three-sixty, seventy-
twenty, ten-eighty. Gravity can wait. You're six
again, you're fighting the whole world, your mom
down there on earth, you in the clouds, Kung Fu
Kid. You leap and twist, your leg slicing through
empty space, splitting the world in two. Wave after
wave after wave, until you have nothing left,
fighting with everything in your heart and mind
and body right up until the very end, when you
hear the gun go off.

INT. GOLDEN PALACE CHINESE RESTAURANT—NIGHT

Kung Fu Guy is dead.

> GREEN
>
> He's dead.

> TURNER
>
> Looks that way.

The Black cop and the White cop regard the prone
Asian male body, partially covered with a sheet.
  A crime scene investigator swabs something.
Another one measures the radius and dispersal
pattern of a pool of drying blood.

> GREEN
> (gazing at the dead Chinese)
> What are we looking at?

> TURNER
> Family drama, probably. Some kind
> of cultural thing.

You open one eye, peek up at Black and White.
  "Hey," Turner says. Off-script.
  "I can't do this anymore," you say.
  Turner smiles. "Yeah, man. I know."
  "See you around, Wu," Green says, pulling you up
to your feet, a dead man now free. "Maybe we can
work together again in the future."
  You close your eyes.

"Hey."

You open your eyes to see Karen leaning over you. Her hair smells so good. She kisses you.

"What now?" she says.

"Looking forward to hanging out with our kid."

Phoebe pounces, knocking the wind out of you.

"Did you win?" she asks.

"No," you say. "I lost."

"Are you dead?"

"Yes. No. I'm not sure."

"Who are you now? Are you still Kung Fu Guy?"

"Nope," you say. "I'm your dad."

"Kung Fu Dad?"

"Just dad."

"Oh," she says. "That's good." She pushes her head into you. Your side feels wet.

"Don't cry," you say.

"But I want to."

"Okay. Cry."

Black and White is leaving town. The cops all filing out. The place is a mess.

You see Old Asian Woman and Karen talking. Uh oh. They approach together.

"We were just talking," your mother says.

"This can't be good," you say.

Old Asian Woman turns to you. She makes that face. Secret pride, maybe. Or bittersweet pain. Little of both.

"You used to jump off the walls. Like a monkey." She asks, "What did you call yourself?"

"Kung Fu Kid," you say. Karen laughs.

Old Asian Woman closes her eyes.

"You always tried so hard at everything, Willis,"
she says. "Maybe I was wrong," she says. "Telling
you to be more."

"I just wanted you and Ba to be happy."

"I was happy. Eating dinner with you. Your
chubby little hand, holding the bowl." You hug her,
kiss the top of her head. It smells just like it
used to. You are not Kung Fu Guy. You are Willis
Wu, dad. Maybe husband. Your dad skills are B,
B-plus on a good day. But you've been practicing.
You say the words. Take what you can get. Try to
build a life. Sometimes, things happen. Mostly they
don't. Sometimes you get to talk. Mostly you don't.
Life at the margins, made from bit pieces.

All the Old Asians, wandering, standing around.
No show. No plot, no world. Just characters. Golden
Palace dismantled. The sky up above. EXT. CHINATOWN.

POST-CREDITS

Miles Turner left the force to attend Harvard
Medical School. He is now a surgeon.

Sarah Green started a singing career. She still
moonlights as a PI.

Green and Turner have started seeing other people,
but they're still friends. And sometimes more.

EXHIBIT B
LAWS OF THE UNITED STATES, PART II

1943   The Chinese Exclusion Act is repealed
by the Magnuson Act and Chinese in the
United States are given the right to become
naturalized citizens, although ethnic Chinese
in America were still prohibited from owning
property or businesses. The quota for Chinese
immigration is set at 105 people per year.

1965   The Immigration and Nationality Act (Hart-
Celler Act) is passed by the 89th United
States Congress and signed into law by
President Lyndon B. Johnson. The law
abolishes the quota-based National Origins
Formula that had been the basis of U.S.
immigration policy since 1921.

*Chinatown, like the
phoenix, rose from
the ashes with a new
facade, dreamed up by
an American-born Chinese
man, built by white
architects, looking like
a stage-set China that
does not exist.*

Philip Choy

ACT VII
EXT. CHINATOWN

MING-CHEN WU

Late one night you see him in the kitchen. With
Phoebe, both of them sitting on overturned plastic
crates, laughing. Wearing one of his shirts from
the seventies. So old that it went out of style,
came back, went out again. On the verge of coming
back around a second time. He was, he is, more
handsome than you. In his eighth decade, enough
thick, black, straight hair to comb back and
across, a clean part on the left side. The way
he first learned how Americans did it, watching
old film reels in central Taiwan, his home now a
distant, watery memory from a Period Piece.

   This stranger, your father. Sifu still in there.
Flickering in and out. There is a dusky, twilit
understanding in his eyes—the gulf inside that he
is slowly falling into. His eyes almost a little
wet. The gulf between the two of you. Permanent
aliens to each other. How many early mornings
and late nights has he spent there? Interior
Golden Palace. He's probably seen it reconfigured,
repurposed, same flimsy walls, a hundred different
stories, five hundred. Same small space. This
place preserved as if in amber. Like a museum,
a presentation of a time and place that always
exist, and never did. A holding cell, purgatory,
a vestibule, the anteroom, the waiting room. It's
in the United States, but not quite America. Some
trick of geography. The story doesn't need to
change, doesn't need to evolve. Because it never
existed. Better if it doesn't. Dinner theater
without a stage. Playing out the same tired old

skit, chopsticks and dragons, Family and Duty, Father and Son. You wondered if it would ever change. You didn't know then what you know now.

Maybe, if you're lucky, she'll teach you. If she can move freely between worlds, why can't you? You watch him for a while. You want to reach out and touch his face. Then someone in the front of the house turns on the karaoke machine, testing testing.

"Dad," Phoebe says. "Are you okay?"

"Yes honey," you say. "Watch this. A-kong is up next."

Ming-Chen Wu takes the stage, smiles. Testing, testing, he says, and he clears his throat, ready to sing about home.

ACKNOWLEDGMENTS

This novel has the tremendous good fortune of being published by the many talented and hard-working people at Pantheon, Vintage, and the Knopf Double-day Publishing Group, including (but not limited to) the following individuals:

CAST

Cover Designer...Tyler Comrie

Text Designer... Anna Knighton

Production Editor.. Kathleen Fridella

Copy Editor ....Fred Chase

Proofreader...Chuck Thompson

Publicist ....Rose Cronin-Jackman

Marketer .... Julianne Clancy

Managing Editor ....Altie Karper

Associate Managing Editor ....Cat Courtade

Publisher Extraordinaire .... Dan Frank

Fancy Pants Imprint ....Pantheon Books

Like many indie productions, making this book was a labor of love. There were many moments of frustration and self-doubt. There were also moments of joy, of shared creation and discovery, thanks mostly to the intelligence and care of:

Executive Producer...Julie Barer

Executive Producer... Josefine Kals

Executive Producer.. Anna Kaufman

Executive Producer...Tim O'Connell

Julie and Tim: this book would literally not exist without your patience, guidance, and extraordinary contributions. (And thanks as well to Nicole Cunningham at The Book Group.)

As evidenced by the epigraphs, certain books were invaluable resources to me in the writing of this novel (in addition to *The Presentation of Self in Everyday Life* by Erving Goffman, a book I will keep rereading until I can't read anymore):

American Chinatown...Bonnie Tsui
San Francisco Chinatown..Philip Choy

For generous financial support provided during the long, sometimes lean, years between books, I am grateful to:

Santa Monica Artist Fellowship.............................City of Santa Monica
Nathan Birnbaum...Cultural Affairs Director

There are certain other people whose support has been essential, both professionally and personally. Having the opportunity to work with people this smart is a privilege, but having them believe in me has been more important than they may realize:

Super Smarty Pants ....Jason Richman
Super Smarty Pants...Mickey Berman
Super Smarty Pants..Mark Ceryak
Super Smarty Pants...David Levine
Super Smarty Pants...Katy Rozelle
Super Smarty Pants...Howie Sanders

The people whose lives and love inspire and motivate me to write:

Mom ....Betty Lin Yu
Dad ....Jin Yu
Daughter ....Sophia Yu
Son...Dylan Yu
The Real Star of the Show..Michelle Jue

ABOUT THE AUTHOR

CHARLES YU is the author of three previous books, including *How to Live Safely in a Science Fictional Universe,* which was a *New York Times* Notable Book and named one of the best books of the year by *Time* magazine. He received the National Book Foundation's 5 Under 35 Award and has been nominated for two WGA awards for his work in television, which includes writing for shows on HBO, AMC, and FX. His fiction and nonfiction have appeared in *The New Yorker, The New York Times, The Wall Street Journal, The Believer,* and *Wired,* among other publications. Yu lives in southern California with his family.

A NOTE ON THE TYPE

This book was set in Courier, a monospaced slab serif typeface designed in 1955 by Howard Kettler. Initially designed for IBM typewriters, it found renewed use in coding, where columns of characters must be consistently aligned, and has also become an industry standard for screenplays.

Composed by North Market Street Graphics, Lancaster, Pennsylvania

Printed and bound by Berryville Graphics, Berryville, Virginia

Designed by Anna B. Knighton